Ladies Ride Out

Kelly M. Cooper

LADIES RIDE OUT

Copyright © 2013 by Kelly M. Cooper

ER Printing & Graphics, LLC
PO Box 181
Dayville, Oregon 97825
info@erprintingandgraphics.com

Chelsey Hill, K.D. Photography

*"I like my friend for what is in her heart,
not for the way she does things."*

–S.K. Lamberson

CHAPTER 1

A slight fog blurred the bottoms of the thick pines along the highway running parallel to the North Santiam River. Marie drove in silence, except for the sounds of the road or an occasional passing car. Her friends slept, Cynthia leaning back in the passenger seat and Mona snuggled in her sleeping bag in the back. They hadn't made a noise since leaving Salem at 4:30 a.m., just twenty minutes after Mona's shift at Salem General Hospital.

Marie pulled off the road to remove her jacket, glancing in the mirror for a moment to admire the new shoulder length cut of her coal black hair. Cynthia stirred, yawned and smiled at her friend.

"Nice hair cut!" Cynthia said, bragging.

"Yea, no one would ever guess you run a hair salon. Look at you, Cyn!" Marie reached over to fold down the mirrored visor. Cynthia's bleached blond hair was pulled up in a plastic clip exposing dark roots, and when she moved it bounced around like a rooster's tail, little straw-like clumps of hair poking out in every direction.

"Who cares?" she said, pushing the visor back up. "We're going to be roughing it in the middle of nowhere for a week. I don't think I need to worry about style right now, Marie!"

Marie pulled back onto the road, the Wagoneer's old automatic transmission shifting hard to make the steep grade.

"Why don't you get rid of this old Jeep? It's not like you can't afford a new car, unless everyone has quit visiting therapists these days!" Cynthia teased.

"Are you kidding?" Her slight New York accent always grew stronger when she talked about her work. "The crazier the world becomes, the more clients I get...besides I can't sell the Jeep, Cyn. It was Max's."

After an awkward pause, Cynthia said, "I need music!" She fussed with the radio until realizing there would be no reception in the mountains. She finally found a CD in the glove box and popped it in, saying playfully, "To set the mood for us!" Martina McBride's 'Wild Angels' shot out of the speakers. She winked at Marie while reaching over the seat to affectionately tousle Mona's short brown hair. Mona pulled the sleeping bag over her head, mumbling a protest.

"Hey, sun's up, sleeping beauty. We're almost there!"

"C'mon Cyn, let her sleep!" Marie insisted as she pushed the stop button on the stereo. Cynthia curled up, leaned against the door and resumed her nap.

* * *

Now that it was quiet again, Marie became lost in thought. She found that driving was therapeutic and, oddly enough, the time when she usually indulged herself in haphazard prayer. She was looking forward to a whole week on horseback in the company of her two best friends.

Since moving to Portland, she had seen less and less of them throughout the year and she missed the camaraderie they had always shared. For that very reason, this year's ride seemed that much more important to her. Marie had always been glad to take charge of planning and booking the rides. Their adventures together had so far included a Wyoming dude ranch, a trip into the Sierras, the Saguaro studded desert of Arizona, and the Rocky Mountains. They had even gone as far as Tennessee, where they swore the mosquitoes were as big as hummingbirds.

For last year's tenth anniversary ride, she had surprised them with custom-made T-shirts that said: "A Woman's Place Is in the Saddle—Ten years and still ridin'." They had always agreed that women who love horses have something special that flows between them, cementing friendships in a unique way that some people found hard to understand. They promised each year to continue the rides as long as they were able. Although Marie had noticed that Mona seemed less enthusiastic about this year's pilgrimage, she hoped it was only her usual moodiness and nurse's 'burn out' causing it. Marie was sure that once out on the trail Mona would unwind and enjoy herself.

* * *

Lying awake under her sleeping bag, Mona was lulled by the hum of the Wagoneer and none too anxious for conversation. Another trail ride, she thought. Secretly she was getting a little tired of these yearly treks and, since her back surgery, wasn't too fond of the pain that was always present after the first day on the ride. She didn't want to let the girls down by letting on that she preferred her own little Arab mare, Lark, and keeping to the local trails or hauling to the coast where she could lope along the beach.

She sighed inwardly, thinking that it just wasn't the same since Marie had moved up to Portland, and she doubted things would ever be the same between the three of them since the ill- fated trip to Mexico three years ago.

Her two friends seemed to be in denial, one of Marie's favorite psycho-babble words. And there was the growing problem between Cynthia and her sixteen-year-old daughter, Heather. Heather was hostile toward her mother and Mona found herself constantly trying to help the two get along. Cynthia had pulled away from her family, and although Mona knew it was unintentional, it wasn't fair to the girl. Whenever Mona attempted to voice her concerns, Cynthia, in her usual style, would make a joke about it and change the subject. Her outward humor, though, didn't fool those close to her; it was a way to mask her pain. Thank God for Bob, Mona thought. Cynthia couldn't ask for a more even-tempered man for a husband. He adored her and was extremely close with his only child, never missing her school functions or swim meets as Cynthia had lately begun to do.

* * *

In the town of Sisters, Marie pulled up to a drive-through espresso, where they all seemed to come alive, chatting with the girl who was making their coffees. The girl had no idea where the town of Willow Forks was but she said they were about an hour from Prineville, which is where they should be able to find out more. Half an hour later they were admiring the Three Sisters peaks while weaving in and out of traffic, trying to find the turn off that would take them east and to the Frost Ranch where they were to begin the trail ride.

The high desert scenery was much different, beautiful in its uniqueness. As they drove along the Ochoco Reservoir where the sun sparkled on its surface, people were on the shore already fishing, and boats were being loaded with kids, dogs and ice chests, ready for a day on the water. Marie explained that while researching Eastern Oregon, she'd read that "Ochoco" was a Native American word for "Red Willow." Cynthia made the comment that she sure didn't see any willows, but there seemed to be lots of those stinking Juniper trees she hated so much.

Mona politely stated that she actually liked the smell herself. "That's because you are around catheters Mona and those trees smell like pee!"

"Good grief Cynthia!" Mona said, rolling her eyes disgust.

* * *

In the higher elevation of the mountains, the pines grew thick and dark, except where a creek would snake along next to the road or through an Aspen-filled meadow. Evidence of past forest fires were on several big slopes, where burned out remains of trees lay about, new growth greening the mountains once again. Guessing they were about an hour from their destination, Marie announced that they were coming up on a rest stop in case anyone had a need. She pulled in and stopped. She and Cynthia rushed to the restrooms as Mona crawled slowly out of the back seat, aching from the cramped position she'd been in. She stretched while standing beside the Jeep and then turned the side mirror out to inspect her face.

"Gawed!" she said out loud.

Cynthia had assured her that the short bobbed haircut would make her look younger. Too bad it hadn't done anything about the tracks of crows' feet marching beneath her thirty-eight year-old eyes. Mona always thought that her one claim to beauty was her green eyes; she hated her big boobs and hefty derriere. Her ex-husband and a handful of other men had said they liked her Rubenesque proportions, but then all men were liars in her opinion. She had a sudden feeling of panic before remembering she had packed her sports bra for the ride. Cynthia had recently suggested she get one to contain those 'bouncing Barbies,' as she referred to Mona's breasts.

After taking her turn in the restroom, Mona returned to find her two friends in a somewhat heated discussion about a bear. "What bear?" she asked.

"There's a bear in the little town up ahead, and Marie won't...." Cynthia tried to explain.

Marie broke in with a slightly patronizing tone. "We don't have time Cyn, maybe on the way home, okay?"

Please mommy, pleeeease!" Cynthia tugged like a child at Marie's sleeve.

"God Cyn, you need your head examined!" Marie twisted

away and opened the driver side door.

"Are you offering me free therapy because I could sure use..."

"Wait a minute," Mona interrupted. "Is this bear in a cage, because that's just cruel!"

"He's in a pen, right Marie? I don't know, shit, I've just never seen a real live bear is all."

"No bear, Cyn!" Marie stated flatly.

"Sorry Mom," Cynthia said.

She turned to wink at Mona, who was again nestled in her sleeping bag, only sitting up this time, shaking her head at the two of them. Marie noticed a faint smile on Mona's face as she looked into the rear view mirror; this made her hopeful.

After several wrong turns onto dirt roads, and much cussing and arguing over the now torn map, they arrived at a ranch entry where a white, cut metal sign hung from a western log archway: "Frost Ranch and Pack Station."

"Shoulda called it Lost Ranch," Mona said in an exaggerated country drawl.

Cynthia threw the map at her and said, "Shut up, you were no help!"

CHAPTER 2

A scrawny little man in a beat up cowboy hat greeted them as they pulled up in front of a turn-of-the-century, two-story house. He introduced himself as "Sully," the gaps between his front teeth causing a whistling sound. "The mithiss iss in the houss, jiss go on in," he said.

Mona shot Cynthia a warning glance, afraid she was going to burst out laughing. "Thanks!" she said and opened her door quickly.

An old border collie lay in the dirt, sunning himself, not even stirring as they approached the house. Another dog came around the corner of the building, barking. A Boxer type, Mona guessed it was. He began wagging his stub of a tail right away and sniffed at her boots

"Rolex!" came a woman's voice from behind the screen. "C'mon in gals!" she said as she opened the door. "I know folks are generally afraid of Pit Bulls, but he's only part, the rest of 'im is Lab. At least that's what the vet thinks."

"Rolex, huh?" Marie said.

"Yep, 'watch dog. He ain't much of one though. Just loves horses and most people." She reached to shake Marie's hand and then the others. "Della Frost," she offered. "Pleased to meet ya."

She was a slight woman with a big smile. A long grey braid ran down her back to her waist. Marie guessed she was around seventy years old.

"Wow, this is a neat house. How old is it?" Marie was admiring the leaded glass in the matching corner cabinets.

"Depends which part, it's been added onto so many times. But I think originally it was built about the time of the Indian wars, and that woulda been around 1880 or thereabouts."

Cynthia ran her hand over the smooth stones of the massive fireplace. It was a masterpiece of craftsmanship, built of materials hauled from a nearby creek. The mantel was a thick juniper log branded in several places with various names the ranch had taken on over the years. The Frosts, they learned, had owned the ranch for thirty seven of those years.

They were ushered into an office off of the living room, where last minute papers were signed as Della began filling them in on things they would need to know. She said they were lucky because late rain had kept the grass green and they would be allowed to have a camp fire. The trail was a little washed out in spots, but nothing to worry about. Their guide, Bev, she insisted, was one of the best, but not much of a "people person." She assured them that they couldn't be in better hands, but that Bev was a little rough around the edges and would take some getting used to.

"She's had a hell of a life, that girl. Don't know what I'd have done without her this season. Mr. Frost up and died on me last winter, and Sully and me, well, we can't run this place just the two of us." She smiled up at them asking for no sympathy. "Bev is at the barn, so I guess we can mosey on down there if ya want."

They followed Della, their boots loud on the wood floors. Cynthia couldn't help thinking about all the people who must have walked across these planks over the years. She was feeling strangely sentimental all of a sudden. A house plant sat wilting on a small table by the front door; Cynthia unscrewed the lid of her water bottle and doused it, the water dripping almost immediately onto the floor. Why did she always feel that whenever she tried to do something nice she always screwed up?

At the barn, Marie parked in a shady spot under a tree and they began unloading their gear. Five horses were tied out, most of them already saddled. Sully was helping a stout woman who could easily have been mistaken for a man. They struggled to adjust the panniers on the pack horse and, when it was secure, Sully walked over to where they stood.

"You've already met Sully here and this is Bev. She'll be your guide for the week," Della said. Bev was bent down under a horse, busying herself with a cinch. She looked up and nodded without making eye contact.

Sully seemed uncomfortable with her lack of manners, glanced anxiously over at Della, and then walked up to Bev. "Here," he said. "Let me do that so's you can meet these ladies!" The guide looked annoyed, her fleshy pockmarked face turning red. She pushed her shaggy hair out of her eyes, folded her arms and stared off to the right as Della awkwardly began introductions. It seemed the woman was unable to look at them. Della forced a laugh, while she explained which horses they were assigned to and filled them in on each horse's particular personality.

Marie would ride a tall black Appaloosa named Ace. He had a spotted rump and thick neck and was what Della called a 'pussy cat.' It was decided that Mona would ride a smaller roan mare, Karza. Why she was on a little horse and petite Marie on a big Appy was a mystery to Mona, but, oh well! Then Sully led a gangly sorrel gelding with a big head and rabbit-like ears over to Cynthia, who immediately burst out laughing.

"Sorry baby!" she said, and stroked his cheek. "Of course this would be my mount for the week, right?" she asked Sully.

He simply grinned then explained, "Now Ma'am, he ain't the purdiest thing, gots a dinosaur head I know. We named him 'Dino,' but he's a gentleman through and through, I guarantee ya!"

"Ha!" came the only comment Bev had made since they had reached the barn. Marie and Mona exchanged questioning glances.

Della quickly began talking to Cynthia about how she used to guide the rides and missed it. "That grey Bev is riding, he's my boy," she said proudly. "I used to cuss the ranchers that used four tracks to move cows and do chores. I'm ashamed to admit that I've resorted to it myself. Workin' horses are gettin' rare these days. And he is one of the best."

As they readied to set out on the trail, Marie, Mona and Cynthia looked at each other with concern. It was as if the three friends were reading each other's minds about the so-called guide, but there was no time now to discuss their feelings.

Maybe, Marie thought, Bev was just a hard woman and would leave them to enjoy their time together. Part of the memories they all shared, though, had been in getting to know the people who lived the life they all envied, living close to the land and building character by those experiences that test one's strengths and weaknesses.

CHAPTER 3

The riders crossed the hay field behind the barn, filing in behind Bev and the pack horse. Sully waited at a big green gate where he sat on the four-track with the dog, Rolex. "You gals have fun and be careful!" he said, when he closed the gate behind them. The dog jumped down, barked once at Sully, then bounded after the riders.

Rolex had a delightful time chasing off into the brush for the next two hours while the group rode in silence. They were tired from the drive over and quiet, apprehensive about the days ahead. Bev glanced over her shoulder on occasion to see if the riders were still in tow. And Rolex, circling back to greet them every once in awhile, seemed more aware of their presence than their guide. The trail had been a slow, steady climb so far, the air still and cool. A hawk held its wings out floating against a perfect blue sky. The day looked promising except for the aloof woman who was such a mystery to the trio of friends.

Soon the heat of the noon day sun permeated the air with the scent of sage and juniper. Rolex dropped down beneath any small bit of shade panting, saliva dripping from his open mouth. Along the trail there were spots where spring water made its way to the surface. The dog lapped at the shallow water and rolled in the mud before bounding off once again to explore. He seemed to have the unlimited energy of a young pup. Bev yelled at him when he ran up beside her horse shaking water all over them and causing the gelding to jump sideways. "Git outa here ya son of a bitch!" Grinning at each other, they couldn't help but enjoy seeing her discomfort. Cynthia had to stifle a laugh with her hand cupped over her mouth.

The trail leveled out where a few big pines cast shadows, a welcome respite from the growing heat. Suddenly Bev pulled her horse up, turned around and said, "We're stoppin' here. Ya got twenty minutes ta eat and whatever. Still three hours from camp."

"O Kee!" Cynthia said in a low voice. She was beginning to feel like they were on a wagon train instead of a pleasure ride.

When Bev disappeared into the trees, Mona turned to the other two and said, "Maybe we should just go back, get a refund and call it good."

"No way!" Cynthia said. "I'm not letting her ruin this for us. It's our tradition, right Marie?"

"This is one shitty trail guide we're stuck with alright!" was her response.

"Ya think?" Mona said. She was sitting on a rock sucking on the little straw in her juice box, thinking that maybe the 'tradition' should be canned.

The horses, tied to nearby trees, stood quietly with their eyes closed, swishing their tails. Marie unpacked the sack lunches Della had prepared for them, roast beef sandwiches that no one seemed to have an appetite for. Rolex was glad to consume the leftovers while they all waited for Bev. They assumed she had taken a trip into the privacy of the woods to relieve herself, but it was now over the twenty-minute limit she had given them. When she finally came stomping out of the shadows, she said nothing to them as she fussed with her saddle bags, tightened her cinch, mounted, and rode on up the trail.

It didn't take long for them to catch up to her, but Cynthia was worried about the growing frustration she saw in Marie. To lighten the situation, she made a goofy comment about the 'camel' she had been assigned to, rocking to and fro in exaggerated motions to the horse's stride. The two friends laughed at Cynthia's comic display while she basked in the secret pleasure that Bev was within earshot.

They found the trail growing increasingly steeper and full of wash outs, requiring all the concentration a rider could muster. The 'ping' of metal shoes against stone and the snapping of the brush that grew out over the trail drowned out most sound. The horses labored hard to make the grade, coughing from the rising dust. Horse sweat, leather and manure filled the air with the aromatherapy that only women who have the love of horses in common can understand.

After a grueling twenty minutes they were on level ground where the horses could take a breather. Up ahead, Bev still wore her coat and crumpled old felt cowboy hat with the dirty brown sweat ring across the front. Mona worried that their guide might topple over from heat stroke since she was dressed as if she were riding through a blizzard. She was talking out loud, either to herself or the horses, and then they heard her singing something inaudible to them—now and then a loud "Ha!" escaping from her mouth.

Cynthia nudged her Tennessee Walker into a shuffling trot to catch up to Marie. "What's up with her?" she asked.

"I don't know, maybe she got bit by a happy bug or something," Marie said.

Behind them, Mona was muttering, "What in the world are we doing headed into a wilderness with this woman as our guide?" when suddenly Bev rode off the trail into a small meadow. She pulled her horses up, looped the lead rope from Molly onto her saddle horn and sat waiting for the others to join her. It appeared to be an unspoken request to stop for a rest, so all three gathered around her in a semi-circle not knowing what to expect. Bev surprised them all by asking, "So, you girls havin' fun yet?" a hint of sarcasm in her gravelly voice.

An awkward silence hung in the air until Marie said, "We always have a good time when we're together."

Bev cackled out a laugh while wiping her brow with the back of her coat sleeve. She looked at each woman for the first time since meeting at the barn.

Cynthia put on a deliberate smile when Bev looked her way and asked, "Do you enjoy guiding, Bev?"

"Huh?" she said, as if caught off guard. "It's a paycheck," she declared.

Cynthia was having fun with this. "I see......nice grey you have there. What's his name?"

"Ain't my horse, belongs to Della. Name's Smokey." She reached down to pat the gelding roughly on the neck. "'Pokey' Smokey. Damn horse got lead in his ass but he packs my fat carcass around anyway," she said in an affectionate tone.

Cynthia felt a small pang of guilt. What childhood trauma, she speculated, might have damaged this hardened woman?

Karza gave a rough shake against the saddle, startling Mona from her relaxed state. Her saddle was loose so she dismounted to tighten the cinch. Bev had noticed too and walked up beside her to help. Throwing the stirrup up over the saddle horn, she pulled the wide leather strap and secured the knot in place. Then she walked around the horse to check the breast and belly straps. "She's a round little bitch, keep an eye on yer cinch," she warned. The smell of strong liquor hung in the air.

CHAPTER 4

There were gullies along the trail and mud puddles that were a particular challenge for Mona's horse, Karza, but with patience and skill she was able to coax her through the water. Bev could be heard singing and talking still, once in a while blurting out, "HA!" This was obviously a habit all her own. Annoyed, Cynthia suggested that maybe Bev was a little "tetched in the head."

An hour or so after their last break, they came to a small clearing where the ground was spongy with moisture, and a stand of Cottonwood trees thrived along a rocky embankment. There were two metal troughs spilling over with water, the source of which they were told was a spring. Bev also informed them that this was their last break before reaching camp. They let their horses have a drink and crop a few mouthfuls of lush green grass before tying them to nearby trees.

Bev had walked off almost immediately, returning a few minutes later to fumble around with the leather bags behind her saddle. She seemed to be forever digging through them even when riding along. The big grin on her face was something new and they exchanged questioning looks. "See that hill over there?" she asked, pointing eastward to a sandy-colored mound with a dark cap. "We call that Squaw Tit. HA!"

Cynthia shaded her eyes from the sun with her hand, and looked in the direction the guide was pointing. "Well now, Bev," she said in a serious tone, "I believe the POLITICALLY correct name for that hill would be 'Native American Breast,' don't you think?"

"Huh?" Bev said, looking puzzled. Then she turned and strode away.

"I think you made her feel stupid, Cyn," Mona said.

"I wasn't trying to!" she swore.

The three of them relaxed in the shade while they waited for Bev to return, bright green confetti-like leaves fluttered above them in the warm breeze. Marie went to her horse and pulled out a bag of beef jerky, dividing it among her friends. They shared small pieces with Rolex, who sat staring at them as if in a trance, drool dripping from both corners of his mouth.

Suddenly a loud popping sound, that could only be a gun shot, shattered the afternoon peace. Everyone jumped to their feet as two more shots followed.

"What the …?" Marie said, while Rolex took off into the bushes barking anxiously. They followed him until they found Bev, her left hand on her hip and a pistol in her right, standing over a dead coyote. Marie stopped next to her, arms folded across her chest. Mona grabbed onto Marie's arm as Cynthia walked past them and bent down over the dog. She reached out to touch the black and yellow mane-like fur on its neck and looked at the eyes, staring in death. Blood was quickly pooling out on the dirt around its teeth, the lips frozen in a snarl. A female, her bulging pink teats lay on the ground beneath her belly. Somewhere, probably in a hole in some dusty bank, her litter of pups would be waiting for her return.

"Saved some rancher a calf, mangy sons' a bitches!" Bev said.

"I like them," Cynthia heard herself say.

Bev stared at Marie with bloodshot eyes, "What? Whad she say?"

"They are survivors....I like that about them," Cynthia answered.

"This un ain't no survivor, lady, yer outa yer friggin' mind! Sneaky bastards is what they are... city people, I swear!" she muttered, as she stomped off.

Rolex sniffed cautiously around the bitch coyote, recoiling every time his nose made contact.

"I don't like it either, buddy," Cynthia said to the dog, as she hugged him around the neck. He whined and licked her face. "You'd think one shot would have made her happy. But no, she had to put three holes in the poor thing." Cynthia stood up, wobbling a little and joined arms with Marie and Mona as they walked back to where the horses waited.

Bev was singing loudly, "On the road again, jist can't wait to git back on the road again..."

Cynthia pulled herself up into the saddle. "Marie?" she asked. "Can't you do something? She's butchering one of Willy's best songs."

CHAPTER 5

The four riders were strung out along the trail in single file, climbing several steep switchbacks before reaching level ground. Molly had rivulets of sweat dripping down her flanks; she swished her tail at the tickling sensation and moaned with exhaustion from the heavy packs. Finally Bev stopped for a five minute break as everyone took a long drink from their water bottles.

"Twenty minutes or so and we'll be in camp," was all she said, popped Smokey on the side with the end of her reins and moved on.

Mona watched the spotted rump of Marie's horse as she became lost in memories of past trail rides she had taken with her friends. The worst had been the one in Montana when they had an encounter with a young grizzly, setting everyone's nerves on edge. Then, they had awakened to six inches of snow, and the temperature had dropped to freezing for the next three nights.

The best memory she had was of the two weeks spent near Wickenburg, Arizona. Heather had begged to come along and Cynthia gave in. At thirteen, her daughter was a pleasure to have along and basked in the attention from Marie and Mona. The desert was beautiful that summer even though the days were hot. Monsoons off the Gulf of Mexico had sent rain storms their way nearly every afternoon. The four of them would sit under the protection of the porch of their little adobe casita, listening to the thunder until the deluge would hit, driving them inside. The windows would rattle and the walls would shake as they screamed and hugged each other in what Cynthia had dubbed 'delightful fright!'

It was a special time for Cynthia and her daughter, too. Mona remembered the trip just the two of them had taken into town for lunch, and to buy Heather her first bra. Even though self conscious, Heather still couldn't resist modeling it in front of them that evening. Mona made a mental note, that the next time she found the right opportunity, to remind Heather about it.

* * *

"I wonder how they ever carved a road into this mountain!" Marie said, looking behind at Mona.

Huge rocks formed a wall on their right; shale littered the trail and spilled down over a cliff into a deep ravine to the left. Mona dismounted to lead Karza through the bad footing.

When Bev turned around to check on them she stopped and yelled, "What's a matter cowgirl? 'Fraid of heights?"

"Everyone's afraid of something, Bev!" Marie hollered at her.

"Zat right?" she said, bobbing her head up and down.

Mona speculated that, at some point, Bev and Marie would lock horns, and knowing that there was a pistol under that shabby coat left her feeling a bit uneasy. Most guides packed a weapon, but most were sober when they were on duty.

* * *

The sun was low when they rode into a meadow of rich green grass; the horses picked up their pace as if getting a second wind upon reaching camp. It looked like paradise to the tired group. Bev tied her horses to the pole corral and headed immediately for the trees.

"Diarrhea?" Mona said, looking at the other two.

"Almost five hours on the trail girls!" Marie said, pointing to her wrist watch.

"I'm stuck to the saddle. Someone has to pry me off!" Cynthia said.

Laughing, they dismounted and began taking care of the horses. Saddles were lined up along the top rail of the corral, saddle bags stacked in a pile, and horses brushed and rubbed down by the time Bev joined them. Marie had already started to unload the packs from Molly, and Cynthia was getting ready to unsaddle Smokey as she came striding toward them. "I kin do that, dammit!"

"I know, Bev, we're just giving you a hand. Jeez!" Cynthia said.

After getting the horses all settled in for the night, they moved their belongings over to the camping area. It was an accommodating site, with logs and rocks forming a sort of crude kitchen around the fire ring. Cynthia began arranging things for dinner on a large, flat rock that served as a primitive counter top. Mona was already spreading their tents out on the grass, along with the hammer and tent stakes. "C'mon Marie, your favorite job," she said.

"Yea right, Mona!" Marie preferred a hammock but was too afraid of bears to risk it.

Cynthia sat down in the shade with Rolex who slept, exhausted from the long day. The air smelled softly of pine needles, damp earth and smoke from the small fire that now burned in the pit. Nearby, a large pool of water welled up in a rocky basin big enough to bathe in, trickling out as a small stream that seemed to disappear into the marshy field below. It was a beautiful, peaceful evening on the mountain. A place to forget the real world and live in the moment—or was this the real world and everything else a fantasy?

CHAPTER 6

Bev draped a blue tarp over the same long post that the saddles rested on to form a make-shift tent. Since arriving, she had kept to herself, talking out loud to the horses and singing to herself, then, suddenly, she was nowhere to be seen. More tired than hungry, Cynthia talked Mona and Marie into soup and crackers for dinner. "We can have a big breakfast tomorrow, but let's keep it simple tonight, okay?" she begged, and they agreed.

Mona spotted Bev at the corral and volunteered to go over and see if she would like something to eat. The guide was leaning with her arms on the top rail and didn't hear Mona approaching in time to hide the whiskey bottle. Mona pretended not to see it, asking if she would like to join them for some soup. Bev turned her head slightly but still didn't answer. Her hair was stuck to her head where her hat had been all day, turned up in a comical flip on each side. Wiping drool from the corner of her mouth with her dirty coat sleeve, she said, "Naw, I ain't hungry. Besides, I got my own food."

"Just thought I'd offer." Mona stood there for a moment wondering if Bev was all right; she felt sorry for the woman, but it was obvious she wanted to be left alone.

It was dusk by the time they finished cleaning up, Cynthia giving the remainder of the soup to Rolex who licked the pan clean. Bev had vanished again. Cynthia heard herself say, "That woman sure wanders off a lot! Wonder if she brought dog food."

"Don't know about that, but she's got liquor on board," Mona said.

"I kinda thought something like that was going on," Cynthia said.

"Great!" Marie stabbed at the fire with a long stick. It popped like a fire cracker as cinders jumped into the air landing on Marie's boot. "Shit!" she yelled, doing a little dance.

Cynthia laughed so hard her eyes watered. Then she felt that dizziness again that the doctor had told her was probably just low blood pressure.

Mona walked off to gather more wood. Away from the light, she looked up and saw a tangerine-colored ball rising up over the hills. "Hey, come see this," she called to her friends. "Did you plan this Marie, I mean, when you booked the ride, did you know there would be a full moon?"

"It just so happens, Mona, they put that information on every calendar a year ahead of time."

"Thanks, that's so like you, Marie," she said, giving her friend a hug.

They hoisted the food packs up into the trees away from wild animals and put things away for the night.

"I need wine," Cynthia said, and went to their tent for the box of Merlot, pouring generous portions into enamel cups. It was finally time to relax and reconnect as friends. The year had been fairly uneventful, except for the fight Cynthia had experienced with Heather two weeks ago. She had been so racked with guilt that she had considered canceling the trail ride. "Here's to lasting friendship!" Cynthia said, raising her cup.

"And here's to a full moon!" Mona added.

Marie closed her eyes momentarily, then said, "Carrots for

Molly who packed this wine all the way up here for us!"

Rolex lay close to the fire, his chin resting on his front paws. He seemed to be listening to their conversation as his eyes darted back and forth between them.

"Pretty good dog for a Pit Bull," Mona said.

"He's only part Pit," Marie corrected.

"Kinda like you, eh Marie?" Cynthia teased.

She broke into a smile. "Yep."

"We still love ya though," Cynthia said, patting her shoulder.

There was a quiet flow of emotion as they sat staring into the glowing embers, a ritual they never tired of. The snapping of the fire and chirping crickets lulled them into temporary silence.

CHAPTER 7

Marie leaned towards the fire, her elbows on her knees. "Catch me up here, Cyn, how's it going with Heather?"

Cynthia scowled. "Are you gonna go 'psycho' on me, Marie?" It was the term she used when Marie would slip into her role as psychologist.

"Nooo. I'm just worried because you have not mentioned your daughter once since we left."

Cynthia wasn't sure she wanted to discuss her feelings, but she knew Marie wouldn't give up until she did. "Well…" Cynthia said, drawing out the word. "Heather went to the Mall Wednesday to get her hair done, instead of coming into my shop. I've always done her hair. Can you believe it?"

"Yes I can. She probably did it to hurt you," Marie said.

"Duh! It worked."

Mona starred intensely at the fire.

"Kids do things like that even when they are on good terms with their parents. I wouldn't take it personally," Marie said.

"She said something weird to me, you guys," Cynthia continued. "We were talking about that Derek kid she's been hanging out with, and I said she should be careful not to hurt Cole. He's been in love with her since sixth grade and assuming, I'm sure, that she's his girl. So, she snaps at me that I'm 'NO VIRGIN'! I started laughing and said, 'That's pretty evident Heather, I gave birth to you, didn't I?' You know what she said?"

"What?" Mona asked, too quickly.

"She said, 'Yeah, I'm my mother's daughter, I guess!' Said she wished she'd never been born. And you should have seen the way she looked at me."

Tears ran down Cynthia's cheeks as Marie gently reached over and laid her hand on her friend's shoulder.

Just then Rolex jumped up, as Bev came stumbling into their midst—drunk. "Roleth, ya goddam traitor!" she bellowed and kicked him hard in the ribs. The dog yelped with pain and disappeared into the dark.

Bev lost her balance. Falling backward, she landed on Mona's lap, where Mona caught her around the waist. Bev began flailing her arms and legs like a drowning person screaming for help. "Lesbians!" she shrieked. "Yer all a bunch of friggin' lesbians!" Reeling, she tried to stand. Mona reached out to steady her. "Don't touch me!" Bev yelled, as she pointed a fleshy finger in her face.

"Whoa, Bev!" Marie said. As she jumped up to catch her, Bev lurched forward, falling toward the fire, her right hand shoved directly into the hot coals.

"Oh my God!" Cynthia cried.

All of them scrambled to pull her out. They dragged her over to a nearby tree and propped her against the trunk. Mona rushed for the first aid kit, yelling at Marie to get some water.

Bev stared at the badly burned hand, mumbling about lesbians and fire. Mona made several attempts to clean the wound, but Bev kept jerking her hand away until Marie finally said, "To hell with her! Let her sleep it off and you can take care of that tomorrow. I've had enough of this crap!" Helping Bev to her feet, they clumsily made their way over to her tent, rolled her inside and walked back to the fire.

"This is exactly what I was afraid of!" Marie said in complaint.

"Lesbians?" Cynthia said, laughing. "She's the one that looks like a dyke."

"The woman definitely has issues," Mona said.

Rolex sat close to the dying embers, looking in Bev's direction and then back at them; he whined as if he were lost.

"Look, he's afraid he'll get kicked again. Poor thing!" Cynthia said.

Marie ignored Cynthia's comment. "Guess we better turn in," she said. "We'll have to figure out tomorrow how we're going to survive this trip."

Cynthia winked at Marie. "C'mon Rolex, you can sleep in our tent."

"Great!" Marie said, and picked up her flashlight.

CHAPTER 8

Awakened by a barrage of curse words and clanging pans, Mona lay in her tent wondering if she was ready to deal with Bev. All night she had dreamed of fire and now she thought about the two little kids who had burned to death in her neighborhood last year. The mother had fallen asleep with a candle burning. Reporters had maligned and hounded the woman until charges were brought against her for the deaths. Two weeks later, she was found in the burned out shell of her home where she had shot herself in the chest.

Shaking off the sudden chill, Mona peeked out from her tent. It was barely light out. She watched Bev attempt to make coffee, her right hand wrapped in a dish towel. Mona decided she should try to help, see if Bev would allow her to treat the burned hand. As she crawled out of the tent, Bev looked in her direction and frowned.

"Morning Bev," Mona said. Coffee grounds were spilled and smoking on the coals, but the pot was bubbling with dark liquid. The first aid kit was still there; Mona began arranging bandages, salve and disinfectant on the flat rock. She filled a pan with water, setting it over the fire to heat, and approached the guide. "Let's have a look at that hand of yours," she said.

Bev stared at her through bloodshot eyes, but didn't protest when Mona unwrapped the makeshift bandage on her hand. Ash and dirt clung to the swollen, red flesh along with fragments of white string from the towel. Mona worried that it might be too late to prevent infection.

"Nasty burn. We really need to clean it up," she said in her best nurse tone while holding Bev's wrist above the burn. The stale smell of yesterday's alcohol filled Mona's nostrils as she led Bev over to the log. Mona felt sorry for the shaggy-haired woman, who now seemed more like a wounded child than a hardened trail guide with the manners of a rattlesnake. "We need to soak your hand, get some of that dirt out, or you'll have infection."

Cynthia and Marie had come out of their tent and were moving around the camp fire, preparing breakfast. Bev sat next to Mona, her hand soaking in a warm Betadine solution; she glared at the two friends who were laughing and playfully dueling with spatulas. Marie came over and put a cup of coffee in Bev's left hand, petting Rolex whose chin now rested on Bev's knee. Strangely passive, she winced only once while Mona dressed and wrapped the wound.

"You some kinda nurse lady, or somethin'?" Bev asked.

Yep, I work in the trauma unit at the hospital."

"Hmm, well, thanks," Bev said.

Cynthia set a plate of bacon and scrambled eggs and some charred potatoes in front of Bev. "What's this?" she asked, pointing to the potatoes.

"Hash blacks. It's a brand new recipe we discovered by accident."

"Well, I ain't eatin' them," she said.

After breakfast Bev retreated to the company of horses while the others tidied up camp and discussed taking a morning ride. When everyone had made a trip to the woods and washed up in the spring, they grabbed snacks and other items for the ride and headed for the corral. Mona found Bev resting her head on her saddle bags, her hat pulled over her face like an old cowpoke.

"We're going out for a short ride, Bev," Mona said. "We'll be back around lunch time."

"Ya want me to catch them horses for ya?" she asked, her voice muffled beneath the hat.

"We can manage. You'll probably want to rest that hand anyway." Mona dug around in her pocket. "I've got some acetaminophen if you want some."

Bev sat up. "A-seed-a-who?" She squinted up into the sunlight, then pushed the hat down on her head and looked up at Mona.

"Tylenol, Bev. I'll put some by the water jug. Help yourself." She turned to walk away.

"Stop motherin' me lady," Bev said to her back.

* * *

Dew glistened on the grass as the riders guided their horses over the meadow and onto the well worn trail. There were small grey rabbits hopping in and out of the underbrush, their little jaws moving back and forth as they chewed. They would stop suddenly and stare with their black, marble-like eyes before scampering off into secret hiding places. A blue jay protested loudly the invasion of his territory, as he swooped down, then up again, to land on one tree after another. Marie joked that she thought for sure they had left Bev back in camp. The angry bird followed the group for a long time before it flew off, apparently satisfied that they were only passing through.

Away from the overpowering presence of their guide, the women relaxed, talking freely, even laughing about the predicament they were in. After last night's incident, they hoped that Bev would pull it together and not spoil the rest of the trip. Discussing it among themselves, they agreed to a plan of action should things get out of hand again.

They found a place to tie the horses and walked out onto a rocky precipice, where the view down into a beautiful valley was nothing less than awe inspiring. The flat topped, mesa-like hills and canyons were awash in morning sunlight. Like the many diverse places they had visited together, Eastern Oregon offered its own unique treasures.

"Is this amazing or what?" Mona said, looking out over the rugged terrain.

"Looks a lot like Arizona," Cynthia said.

"I take pictures of things like this, but when I look at them later...it's not the same." Mona focused her digital camera and snapped a few shots.

"Smell that!" Mona said, drawing in a deep breath through her nose. The scent of sage and juniper was heavy in the air.

The three women walked back to their horses, arm-in-arm, silent except for the crunching sound of their boots on the gravel.

CHAPTER 9

Thrilled to see a bobcat that didn't seem a bit disturbed by their presence, they waited in the shade of a tree for him to wander out of sight. Mona had zoomed in with her camera and taken several close-ups of the small cat.

"As long as we don't see a cougar, I'm good," Cynthia said, as they took up the trail again.

"Or a bear," Marie added.

By one o'clock, everyone agreed it was time to head back for some lunch. After circling the horses around the back side of the rocky hill that bordered the corrals, they approached camp. Rolex came bounding up to them—a piece of shredded rope hung from his collar.

"Uh, oh! Rolex is in big trouble," Cynthia said.

At the corral all was quiet, and Bev was nowhere to be seen. Dismounting, Cynthia took the piece of rope off of Rolex's collar; she cut a new piece and retied it to the fence post. The dog moved happily amongst the horses as if being of some help, then went over and stuck his head inside Bev's tent.

"Git outa here! Who turned the damned dog loose?" Bev yelled.

"I did," Cynthia said, winking over her saddle at Marie.

The horses took turns rolling, shook off the dirt that clung to the sweaty spots, and drank generously from the trough. They were given a small portion of grain and some baby carrots from Mona's saddle bags. Not to be left out, Molly and Smokey crowded in for a share, causing a scuffle that almost got Mona kicked.

"City girl! If ya don't stop spoiling them horses, yer gonna git yer head kicked off!" Bev said from where she now sat on a stump.

Mona made no reply; the agreement between her, Cynthia and Marie was that they would not feed into Bev's goading, hoping, of course, to maintain peace for the next five days.

"We're gonna make some lunch, Bev. Are you hungry?" Cynthia asked.

"Naw."

"I can bring you a sandwich," she offered.

"I ain't helpless, dammit!" Bev said with a snarl.

* * *

In the quiet afternoon, with only the sounds and scents of nature surrounding them, the women sought out privacy, each in their own way. Mona had hiked up onto the rocks above camp, and Cynthia was in the corral brushing the horses. Marie lay in her tent reading a cheap romance she had brought along. She was thinking that she must be entering some new phase of menopause, because even the steamy parts of the novel did nothing but threaten to put her to sleep. The sun warmed the inside of the tent; a breeze pushed lightly through the mesh flap. Marie felt like a baby resting in its crib. A baby...Maxwell. Why was it she always thought of Max when she was feeling the most content?

CHAPTER 10

Taking care of Maxwell had become Marie's life work. It was what brought her the most satisfaction, seeing him grow from a nursing infant to a young man she was proud of. When she found out she was pregnant, her boyfriend expected Marie to have an abortion, said he wouldn't have any 'swell bellies' around. That's when Marie realized she lacked respect for the man to begin with and now, instantly, she had none. He walked away that day without ever contacting her again.

At twenty nine, Marie was ready for motherhood and, if she had to do it alone, she would manage. She finished school and immediately landed a good job, taking night classes and working hard until obtaining a masters' degree in psychology. Finally able to establish her own practice, Marie had made the move from Salem to Portland. Through it all, she had put Max first and felt very lucky to be able to give him everything he needed, even as a single mom.

Max was around eleven years old when he began harping on her to date, have a life of her own, he said, as if he were a grown-up and knew about these things. Marie tried several times, almost giving in to two marriage proposals. But, she found she was very content to call Max and herself a family. Her biggest fear was that a man might come in and upset the tranquility she had worked so hard to preserve. The other thing she worried about was a guy physically abusing Max, knocking him around the way her own stepfather had done.

On graduation night, Max's face was lit with pride as he picked Marie up from the folding metal chair in the auditorium and twirled her around. The chair nearly toppled over when he sat her back down. "Show off!" she yelled at him. He blew her a kiss, his grey eyes penetrating a place in her soul she had never known existed until that moment.

Marie tossed and turned that night, a movie of their life together for the past eighteen years playing in her head. There had been no dad around when Max kept her up all night with colic or an earache, or when he skinned his knees riding his first bike. She never asked his father for anything and had seen him only once; that was when Max was almost nine years old. They were Christmas shopping in the Mall when she heard a voice behind her that caught her attention. When she turned around, he was standing there in front of her, his arms around a big breasted, blond 'Barbie' in stiletto heels.

"Hello Greg," she said. He introduced his partner who opened her mouth wide, her thickly glossed lips parting to reveal a full set of perfectly capped teeth. Of course he would want that of his woman, Marie was thinking.

"This is my son Maxwell," she said with obvious pride.

"Looks just like you 'Ria," he said in a condescending manner.

He was the only one who had ever taken the liberty to shorten her name like that, always making her feel like a child. It was unhealthy, she knew, but if there was a hell, Marie hoped Gregory McDowell would spend at least an hour there.

Before drifting off into a fitful sleep, Marie remembered Max's promise. They were going to a party at the beach house of a friend after graduation, but they would be safe. Everyone was sleeping over, and there would be no drinking and driving. She wished they weren't drinking at all, but she also knew kids would find a way, no matter how much supervision was imposed on them. Parents of some of the other kids were camped on the beach that night and would be checking on them periodically.

Every time Marie tried to recall those first few days, they swam in her head like a murky stream, through which she could make out only part of the details. She thought more would come to her later, but nothing ever surfaced, having been washed away along with all the debris of her once ordinary life.

She remembered the police at her door in the early morning light. "Max dead...Ecstasy?" Marie's voice sounded hollow in her own ears. "But, that's not... possible, officer. You see, I'm a therapist. Max....Max would never take that drug."

The men were visibly uncomfortable with her reaction, looking at each other uneasily. Had she been hysterical, it would have made more sense. They asked if there was a Mr. Geraci. She said no, but that they should call Mona. She recited the number to them then went to the kitchen to make coffee.

* * *

Bob and Cynthia were in her living room, the police talking quietly with them. Mona wasn't there; she was probably working. Max was dead. Marie wanted to see him, and she did. And then there was a funeral, followed by long weeks where she sat on her bed crying. Nights—when the only arms wrapped around her were her own, as she rocked away at the pain. Often, she would wake up in Max's room, her face pressed into his pillow. She would breathe in the scent of him, trying to remember. She wanted to take back all the times when she'd told grieving clients that they shouldn't be alone. Now she knew first hand what sorrow could do to an otherwise happy human being. When you hit the ground hard, sometimes you just wanted to stay there all by yourself for awhile, until you felt like you could put your legs beneath you once again. Stand up and look into the faces of the people who felt sorry for you.

* * *

The book that lay on Marie's chest threatened to suffocate her, before she realized it was the memories that weighed heavily on her heart and not the paperback. So much for resting, she thought. Wiping the tears from her eyes, she looked at the book's cover, where a woman in a flowing dress, her breasts bulging, was wrapped in the arms of a dark-haired rogue. She wondered how people could read this stuff.

When she peeked out of the tent, Marie saw Cynthia holding lead lines as Ace and Karza grazed happily on the other side of the marsh. She heard Bev's loud "Ha!" from where she and Mona sat perched high on the rocky hill above camp. After splashing water on her face, Marie pulled her hair through the hole in the back of her Oregon Beavers' cap to form a short pony tail. Waving at Cynthia, she started hiking up the rocks toward Mona and Bev, hoping to shake off the sadness that still lingered.

CHAPTER 11

As Marie approached Mona and Bev, she found it amusing that they were chatting away like old friends. Bev grew silent and looked annoyed when Marie sat down on a nearby rock.

"Hey, mind if I join you? I woke up, found the camp deserted and got scared," she joked.

Ignoring Marie, Mona continued the conversation she was having with Bev. "So, could you get on with a pack station around there?"

"In the Sierras somewhere maybe, I worked up in 'em mountains once," she said. There was a long silence; Marie saw what looked like tears forming in the guide's eyes. "I can't live in Modesto no more, and I sure as hell ain't livin' with my mom. I gotta think on it. Della needs me for now, but I don't want no charity!" She stood up and grabbed her old coat which she had been sitting on. She rolled down the sleeves of the western style shirt she had on and snapped the cuffs at her wrists. Squinting against the overhead sun, she pointed to the west with her bandaged hand. "Got some rain comin' in girls, see there?" Along the bottom of the skyline an ominous, dark grey strip lay like a distant highway.

"But," Marie said, "I checked the internet before we left, and it said partly cloudy for today and tomorrow."

"Ha! Jist remember, what happens in the valley ain't necessarily what happens on the mountain," Bev retorted.

"I'll keep that in mind," Marie said, irritated by Bev's attempt at humor.

Rolex came scrambling up the rocks panting, long strings of slobber hanging from his mouth. He greeted each of them then shook, the saliva landing all over Marie's right arm.

"Dammit, Rolex!" Her face wore a look of disgust as she pulled a bandana from her pocket to wipe it off.

"You allergic to dogs or somethin', lady?" Bev asked, a big smile across her face. It was obvious she was enjoying this.

Mona quickly stood up and said, "Better get moving I guess if we're having those steaks tonight." She and Bev had gathered their things and were already heading down the narrow trail with Rolex in the lead.

* * *

Marie stayed behind, feeling as if she had invaded their space somehow. Hurt by being brushed off so easily by Mona, she sat there wondering why she had bothered to hike all the way up this hill just to receive another dose of Bev's sarcasm. And now she and Mona seemed to be best buds, but then Mona was always taking someone under her proverbial wing. Marie decided that if it made the rest of the week go smoothly, it might be a good thing that Mona had befriended their guide.

Marie sat quietly absorbing everything around her. There was something about being out here among the elements that made her feel childlike and vulnerable. The thought occurred to her that pioneer women had come through this area, and some had survived great losses along the trail trying to achieve their dreams. Marie had read that more often it was the dream of getting married and the women had agreed to come along in the hope that their new life would be all that they had been told it was out west. All she knew for sure is that she admired their courage and felt a kindred spirit in those strong women.

She looked up. Had she been sitting there so long? The sun was hanging low in the west above a blackening sky; it did, indeed, look like rain was coming their way. Marie stood up, stretched, and rubbed her sore bottom where the rocks had dug into her flesh, then slowly made her way down off the hill. She was determined to give Bev a wide berth and enjoy the evening in spite of the guide's sharp tongue.

* * *

The grilling steaks sent up an enticing aroma, ranch style beans bubbled in a pan, and ears of corn wrapped in foil were roasting over the fire. It would be a feast among friends, which Marie now guessed included Bev, the formerly 'outcast' trail guide. She had stayed away from the bottle all day as far as Marie could tell and might just be tolerable to have around.

They filled their plates and insisted that Bev join them, which she reluctantly accepted. Not bothering to cut up her steak, she held it in her left hand, the juices running into the sleeve of her coat. Dipping the steak into the beans, she tore off big chunks with her teeth, then polished off two ears of corn and belched. Cynthia giggled when Marie's face contorted into a prune; even Rolex had better manners she was thinking. Mona was talking with Bev as Marie struggled to find something that could warm her to this coarse woman. And then a memory popped into her head, something she tried to ignore but couldn't.

The December before he died, Max came home after volunteering at the homeless shelter, along with some other kids from his sociology class. They had served Christmas dinner to the winos and tent city dwellers, but Max acted like he had just returned from a rock concert. He was filled with pure joy from the experience, which surprised Marie. He talked about the homeless in the weeks that followed, quick to spot the sad cases that filed in among Salem's average population.

"Look Mom!" he would say as they were driving along. He would point to some disheveled human being huddled under a bush or pushing their lives around in a shopping cart.

"You can't save them, son," she told him. "Most of these people have made choices that put them where they are."

Max stared out the window for a few moments before he said, "Mom, do you feel the same way about the people you are trying to help?"

Marie knew it was a fair question, but she also realized she wasn't able to give him the answer he needed. Her patients were a class of people who avoided eye contact with the homeless. Wealthy citizens willing to fork out plenty of money to have a professional tell them what they already knew and weren't really willing to do anything about. They took yoga classes, vacations and prescription drugs to fill the holes in their souls, only to return empty week after week for more therapy. On her worst days, Marie longed to be back at the women's prison, where she had been required to put in three hundred hours as a counselor, one of the requirements she had to fulfill to obtain a Masters degree in Psychology.

"I wanted to be a ballerina. Ha!" It was Bev's voice that jerked Marie back to the present. She couldn't believe what she was hearing...ballerina.

CHAPTER 12

"A ballerina!" Cynthia said.

"Yep. But I was too fat and clumsy. My uncle went an' bought me a stick horse. I been ridin' ever since. Near as I can count, I've worked for nine different outfits," Bev said.

Marie wondered if maybe Bev had trouble keeping a job, but knew better than to voice her thoughts.

"I asked Steve when he was walking out on me what he wanted to be when he grew up," Mona said. "I don't think he found any humor in the question though."

"What did you want to grow up and be when you were a kid?" Cynthia asked Mona.

"A nurse!" she said. They all laughed.

"Marie wanted to be an airplane pilot, but she hates to fly now, right Marie?" Cynthia said.

"Pretty much," Marie said.

"Marie lost two colleagues in one of the planes that hit the Twin Towers," Mona explained to Bev.

"I didn't even know 'bout it until two days after it happened. I was out in the middle of Montana, helpin' gather cows. We rode into the Rockin' B Ranch and the place looked like a ghost town.

Everyone was inside watchin' the TV," Bev said.

Cynthia was leaning with her back against a tree; she held one knee with her hands, her fingers entwined. "That was a sad day in America," she said.

"Yep." Bev nodded her head in agreement.

Marie swiveled and leveled her gaze at Cynthia. "Okay, Cyn, cough it up. What did you want to be?"

"Not a hairdresser I can tell you!" Cynthia laughed.

"What then?" Marie said.

"Guess I just wanted to get married and have babies," she said.

Bev looked uncomfortable as she got up, saying she was going to check on the horses and then 'hit the hay.'

"Good night Bev," Mona called after her. "I wonder if Bev has ever had a man or kids," she whispered to Cynthia.

The air was growing colder as a breeze came up, scattering ashes along the ground. In the distance, lightning flashed against the darkness. Marie went to her tent for the wine and a jacket, returning with her stash of canned Pirouette cookies.

"Here's to a day of no drama," Marie said, handing the wine to Cynthia. They huddled close to the fire, Cynthia in the middle covered with a bright-colored blanket. Mona commented that she wished she had re-dressed Bev's hand before she had gone off to bed.

"Mmm, these are good, Marie!" Cynthia said.

"That's because they are Italian. Isn't that the blanket...?" Marie started to ask.

"That I got in Mexico? Yes. It was made in Peru, though," Cynthia said. The blanket had a mix of red, purple and yellow blocks, with stick-figured humans and llamas marching in rows above a Peruvian Indian design. Cynthia fingered the white cotton fringe on the edge, her eyes glossy.

"Did you eat Cyn, I didn't see you eat?"

"I ate!" she swore.

"You seem tipsy to me."

"Why do you keep that thing anyway, Cyn?" Marie asked.

Cynthia turned to look at Marie with her eyes wide and said, "Penance, I guess. You know all about penance, being Catholic, right?"

Marie was momentarily quiet, wondering how to respond. "Cyn, I wish you wouldn't get like this. I lost a child, too, don't forget." Her tone was deliberately somber and measured. But she ached just the same.

"You didn't kill Max though, did you?" Cynthia asked, her eyes filled with tears.

Marie knew there was no use talking to Cynthia tonight. No matter what she said, it would be wrong. She hated it when Cynthia would beat herself up like this, expecting her friends to join in her self-loathing.

"I'm going to bed," Marie said. She poured her wine on the ground and looked at Mona pleadingly. The exchange was familiar between them, and Marie knew that Mona would stay with Cynthia until her mood improved. Mona's arm was around her, the two of them staring at the glowing log. Strands of loose hair were whipping around Cynthia's head in the wind. Walking away from them, Marie followed the beam of her flashlight toward the tent. She thought Cynthia had aged recently and the 'funny girl' side of her personality had nearly disappeared. For the second time that day Marie felt a great sadness envelope her.

CHAPTER 13

It had been five years since the ill-fated trip to Mexico that was still haunting their friendship. Marie wondered if Cynthia would ever move past what she referred to as the 'Big Cyn, Sin'. Marie couldn't sleep thinking back over all the details. She remembered that Cynthia really hadn't wanted to go, feeling guilty about leaving Bob and Heather behind. Bob had promised that their daughter would be perfectly happy at summer camp and would hardly know her mother was away. Cyn also needed a break from work, he insisted. They had decided to fly down instead of taking a cruise, leaving from Seattle then changing planes in San Francisco, before arriving in beautiful Puerto Vallarta.

She remembered calling Cynthia at work, excited about the idea.

"We're going to Mexico!" Marie said.

"What? I'm doing a color, can you make it quick?" Cynthia replied.

"We can ride on the beach and soak up the sun. It's a perfect compromise, Cyn. Mona's back needs a rest anyway. What do ya think?"

"You are crazy, call me later." Cynthia laughed as she hung up the phone.

Admittedly, something just hadn't felt right from the beginning. Marie was convinced that it was the break from their traditional trail rides. But Mona wasn't up to a ride having just gone through back surgery, and Marie had managed to get them a super deal on the vacation package.

Tonight she felt a new pang of guilt, knowing that she was the one who had wanted to experience Mexico and had selfishly pushed for it.

* * *

There were street dances with dark men in sombreros, whirling beautiful women in bright, flowing skirts. The three friends shopped, ate and drank more than they could ever remember. It was nothing like their usual times together. They spent late mornings lounging around the pool, meeting other tourists and nursing headaches. One afternoon, Cynthia and Marie had taken a ride along the beach on some malnourished horses, deciding not to take advantage of that again.

On their fourth day in Puerto Vallarta, Cynthia stayed behind to read a book at poolside, while Mona and Marie took a walk along the beach in search of shells. Basking contentedly in the sun on a cot, Cynthia thought about her husband. As her eyes closed, she tried to remember when she had last felt any romantic feelings toward him. She had long ago realized that, over the years, Bob had become more of a friend than a lover. He was a good man who cherished her; what more could a woman ask for? It wasn't that she didn't love him, but the romance had definitely taken a back seat over the past decade. What had happened, she wondered? Marie often warned her that "Cinderella isn't real!" Marie had watched too many good marriages end because people had unreal expectations. She believed that things like loyalty, patience, and what she referred to as 'stick-to-it-iveness' made for lasting relationships.

Suddenly, Cynthia felt as if she were being watched. Opening her eyes, she saw a man just a few feet away; he was staring at her all right. When their eyes met, he smiled and got up from his chair.

"My name is Jon," he said as he approached. He was tall and good looking, with short blond hair and a trim mustache. His eyes were as blue as the ocean waters just yards away, but his body was also as pale as the sand. Cynthia let out a laugh that she couldn't stifle. The man withdrew the hand he had extended and looked at her curiously.

"Sorry!" Cynthia said. "It's just that you don't look like you've spent much time in the sun."

"As I said, my name is Jon. I am Canadian, on holiday. And your name…?"

"Cynthia, my friends and family call me Cyn," she said, taking his soft hand in hers.

"Can I get you something to drink?" he offered.

"Nope. Been doing far too much of that as it is." Cynthia sat up. She started to pull her towel around her, but then felt giddy from the looks this man was giving her. She decided she rather liked the way his eyes roved over her body, making her feel like twenty again.

The two chatted about their lives, leaving out details each felt were best left unsaid. This was nothing new, an old game played out over thousands of years by members of the opposite sex. And when Marie and Mona found them talking by the pool, they saw nothing unusual about it, inviting Jon to join them for dinner and margaritas later that evening.

"Jon is a doctor!" Cynthia told them after he had begged off to take a nap in his room.

"So?" Marie said.

"Probably a gynecologist," Mona said.

"How did you know?" Cynthia said.

"I was just kidding, Cyn. Are you serious?"

"What's wrong with that?" Cynthia asked, sounding surprised.

"Great! He will be examining us over dinner, that's gross!"

Marie laughed then dove into the pool.

* * *

That evening, Marie was growing tired of hearing about Jon's divorce and financial settlement with his ex-wife, when Mona asked if she was ready to go back to the room.

"What about you, Cyn? We're going snorkeling first thing in the morning. Better get some rest."

"I'm gonna have one more drink then I'll be there, 'kay?"

"Suit yourself," Mona said.

* * *

The door opened quietly. Marie looked at the red numbers on the alarm clock: three forty-seven. Cynthia went straight to the bathroom, where she showered for over twenty minutes. Just as Marie was getting ready to check on her, she emerged from the bathroom and walked over to the couch where she curled up and soon began to snore.

It was after nine a.m. the next morning before Cynthia woke up with a pounding headache and found the note left on the dresser: Marie and Mona had gone with their snorkel instructor and would meet her for lunch in the plaza.

Cynthia stayed in their room, afraid she might run into the Canadian but, by one o'clock she was starving. Hoping that Marie and Mona had returned, she left the room in search of them. At the bar, she ordered a non-alcoholic drink that the bartender promised would cure any hangover. It was an icy, green melon-flavored thing that gave her freeze-brain when she drank it too fast. Sitting in a dark corner behind a tall, leafy plant, Cynthia held her head in her hands, saying to herself, "Oh my God!" over and over.

Then Jon came into the bar, looked around without spotting her and left. Only moments later, Marie entered the plaza and Cynthia could hear her in that nasal, New York accent asking if the bartender had seen their "little blond friend with the spiked hair cut." He pointed to Cynthia in the corner and set them all up with drinks, then brought chips and salsa to their table.

"No thanks!" Cynthia said, as a frosty margarita was placed in front of her.

"What's up with you, Cyn?" Mona wanted to know.

"Yeah, out with whatever-it-is, because I can't deal with this weirdness," Marie said in an anxious whisper.

Cynthia stirred the straw around in her empty glass for a long time, then sat back with her arms folded across her chest. "Well...I...kinda slept with Jon...you know, that Canadian."

"You, what?" Marie said, not believing what she was hearing.

"Kinda? Kinda? Oh, Cyn!" Mona said, shaking her head.

CHAPTER 14

The two sat quietly by the fire, ducking their heads as the wind began swirling smoke in their eyes. They assumed that Bev was asleep in her tent and were waiting for the coals to burn down so they could dowse them with water. Mona could hear the horses moving restlessly over in the corral as the lightning flashed increasingly closer, bringing with it the fresh smell of rain. A sudden crack of thunder made Cynthia jump and let out a little squeal as she clung to Mona. Rolex got up, made a circle around them and then curled up in a ball once again, close to the warm rocks of the fire ring. He had just begun to relax when Bev appeared in the dim light of the embers, causing the dog to jump up and back away. She took one look at Cynthia and Mona, pointed, and started laughing. It was evident that she had indulged herself in a large dose of liquor again.

"I knew it!" she said, shaking her finger at them.

"Don't even start, Bev," Mona said, her tone challenging.

After glaring at them for a few moments, Bev turned away, picked up a large chunk of wood and dropped it on the dying fire, sending ashes and sparks into the wind. The log flamed up and Bev said, "Ha!"

"We were going to let that go out," Mona said. She stood up. A few big drops of rain hit their cheeks and hissed on the fire.

Cynthia stood too, grabbing her blanket. "Might start a range fire there, Bev, if yer not careful," she warned. She gave Mona a wink. Mona just shook her head. Resigned, they left the guide to tend the fire and made their way to the shelter of their tents.

"Good night, Cyn," Mona said.

"'Nite, John Boy," she replied.

Sometime around midnight the pain in Mona's back woke her up, so she decided to check on the fire. Walking out far enough to get a good look, she spotted Bev leaned up against the log bench, her chin on her chest. The fire was out and Rolex, trying to keep warm, was curled up between Bev's sprawled out legs. Mona went back to her cozy bed and tried to sleep. Before long, the rain started to come down and she heard Bev cussing in her usual manner as she scrambled for shelter. Mona smiled to herself, thinking that Bev deserved a good cooling off after all she had done to mess up their ride. She lay listening to the rain, dozing in and out of sleep.

* * *

"Are you awake?" Marie whispered as she unzipped Mona's tent flap.

"Most of the night, as a matter of fact," she answered.

"It rained pretty hard. Do you still want to ride this morning?" Marie asked. "It's really pretty out."

"I don't know. What about Cyn?"

"She wants to stay behind, headache, I guess. Is she okay, did you talk to her?"

"Not much chance to, we had another visit from Bev. Apparently she has a cache of liquor hidden away somewhere," Mona said.

"Good reason to get out of here for a while. Leave the crusty ole' broad alone, she probably won't wake up for hours," she said.

Marie gave the horses a small helping of hay pellets while

brushing and saddling. The sun was shining between clumped grey clouds; water dripped from the trees and plopped down on her as a bird landed on the limb above. Marie received what she guessed was at least a cupful on her head, when she looked up and spotted a jay that seemed delighted to have given her a morning bath.

"Go away you little demon!" She picked up a pine cone and threw it at him.

"Abusing little birds I see," Mona said from behind her.

"Yah, well I've already been baptized," Marie said.

"Breakfast," Mona said, handing her a steaming cup of coffee and a PopTart.

* * *

Even after an hour out, Karza was still skittish as they made their way along the muddy trail. She froze when a covey of quail crossed in front of them. The mare seemed to think every rock and bush was a monster.

"Hope we don't have a rodeo," Mona said, after her horse snorted and sidestepped at a leather glove on the trail.

"You worry too much, Mona," Marie said.

"Yeah, well I have this back thing, you know. I always feel safer on Lark."

"Maybe next time, you should bring your own horse then."

Mona stuck her tongue out at Marie.

CHAPTER 15

By ten o'clock they had been riding for over an hour, when Marie noticed a narrow road leading off to the right which ran parallel to a small creek they had just crossed. A wire gate was pulled to the side where it leaned against a tree. There were no signs to warn against trespassing, and no indication that anyone had been on the road recently.

"What do you think, should we check it out?" Marie asked.

"Isn't it all public land up here?" Mona wanted to know.

"I'm not sure, Bev has the map."

"I say we go ahead and explore it anyway," Mona said.

Numerous puddles pooled on the road, the mud slippery, but they were on flat ground as they rode on, quietly savoring the beauty around them. Wet earth and pine scent filled the air as the sun burned off the morning mist. The rain had moved east toward Aldrich Mountain, where grey clouds hung ominously over the peaks.

Descending into a low spot where they met up with the creek again, they came upon a copse of cottonwoods thriving in the moist soil. The horses weren't a bit interested in water, wanting only to nibble on the tender grass along the bank. Mona let the little roan's head down.

"You are getting lax with your trail manners," Marie warned.

"Nah, I think I'm getting old, reliving my childhood or something. I dare someone to slap me on the hand when I reach for a cookie!"

"Rebel," Marie said, as she gave Ace his head to graze.

Mona turned her face toward the sun. Tilting her head back, she closed her eyes and said, "Smells like peace. I wish I could save moments like this, take them out when I feel overwhelmed. I'm so tired of taking care of everyone's wounds."

"You never show it." Marie said. "You've got to stop hiding your feelings, girlfriend."

Mona gave her a warning look.

"Sorry, sorry!" Marie said. "C'mon, give me that camera and I'll get a picture of you having a moment."

"Nope, you ruined it," Mona said flippantly as she pulled the mare's head up. "We better see where this road leads, if anywhere."

Marie clucked at the big appaloosa and moved him up alongside Karza. They hadn't gone far when Mona put up her hand and said, "Hear that?"

Marie strained to listen as they both stopped. The horses were impatient to keep moving.

"Shh," Mona said to the mare, now tossing her head, the bridle making a clanking noise. She stroked Karza's neck.

A voice was whooping and hollering somewhere off in the distance.

"Oh God, it's probably Bev coming to find us. I think your peace is about to be stolen," Marie complained.

"No, listen."

There was another sound, that of a motorized vehicle. Now Mona was secretly wishing it had been Bev, because it was hard to tell who might be making such a racket.

"What should we do?"

"Head back I think, try to avoid whatever fools are out there."

Marie squeezed her legs against Ace's sides, taking the lead up the slope and onto the road leading back out. Their horses' ears had picked up on the foreign sounds, twitching curiously. The two pairs rode side by side, stopping several times to try and pinpoint the source of their irritation. They came around a turn and immediately moved off to the side. Several vehicles had slowed to a stop on the muddy road, just as they pulled the horses up.

An older army jeep was in the lead, followed by three four tracks, all painted in camouflage. The driver of the jeep had raised his hand in some kind of signal to alert the men behind him. Why are they using camo, Marie wondered, if they are making so much noise? The group looked like a comical bunch of hunter types to her, but, she could see that Mona was extremely uncomfortable.

The apparent leader now stood up, in a commanding stance not unlike the photos of Adolf Hitler that Marie remembered from her history classes. He held the barrel of a shotgun, its butt resting on the seat of the jeep. His head was shaved and a red bandanna was tied around his neck; he was dressed in a camouflage coat. Marie guessed his age to be around forty.

They had expected the group to drive by. But no, they had killed their motors, and seemed to be enjoying the fact that they had come upon the riders. Two men with long dirty beards and stocking caps passed a whiskey flask between them and licked their fat, red lips, then elbowed each other and laughed. "Hee hee!"

"Well, well, well. Would ya look at what we got here, boys," the leader said as he pulled at the bandana and rolled his head. "Two little fillies out frolicking in the woods." He seemed quite impressed with his own cleverness when he drew chuckles from his audience.

Marie whispered to Mona, "Don't let him intimidate you."

"Whadya say woman?" he asked Marie, as he jumped out of the jeep without opening the door.

He was wearing a filthy set of leggings, riddled with holes. She deliberately ignored him, scanning the group of men to see if there might be someone among them with a conscience. A young man, who Marie guessed to be in his early twenties, seemed out of place compared to the others. He wore a black tee shirt that read 'Born to Die' across his chest, the bulging muscles of his arms tanned and tattooed. The silver Celtic cross around his neck glittered in the sun sending splinters of light in all directions. When their eyes met, he looked down, like a dog does when it's done something wrong. She thought of Max and wondered what this kid was doing here with these thugs. It angered her with a mother's passion.

"We're camped right over this ridge." She pointed west. "Our guide is scheduled to meet up with us where the main road connects with this one," she said, trying to keep her voice calm. This man, who seemed to be in charge, she knew from experience, was likely a coward and a dangerous bully, but a leader nonetheless.

"I didn't see no camp back 'er, did you boys?" He leered at Marie and grinned, with a set of rotten, broken teeth.

"Nope, naw, ugh ugh," came their replies.

"Well, that's where we're headed, back to camp," Marie said. "Mona, let's go." They nudged their horses forward only to have the bully grab Karza's reigns, pulling them to a stop. The mare tossed her head nervously, trying to rear as he jerked on her bridle.

"Moaan...ah," he said, flashing his studded tongue at her as the others laughed. He put his hand on her thigh and squeezed it. Mona looked down at his dirty fingernails and shuddered. He spat a stream of brown tobacco juice onto a rock then wiped the drool from the corner of his mouth.

CHAPTER 16

Marie quickly maneuvered Ace behind Mona, forcing the man to step back. That's when she noticed the pistol strapped to his chest beneath his coat. Standing up to his ankles in water and angry at Marie's bold move, his jaw twitched and his beady eyes bored into her. She returned his glare and stood her ground. A sudden grin covered his face as he pulled again at the bandana and rolled his head in the same curious way. Marie prepared herself, sensing that he was a time bomb ready to go off.

"No weddin' rings? Zat mean yer up for grabs, girls?" he asked. One of the bearded men whistled. "We know this is little Moan...ah, but we need to know yer name, too, right boys?" He looked to his cronies for approval.

Marie had a sick feeling in her stomach and then she suddenly felt like laughing hysterically. Birds were twittering in the trees, the clouds soft against a perfect blue sky on this ordinary summer morning—while at the same time these vile men held them in their power. Was this not a glimpse of the insanity of the world they were trying to escape? The very reason they'd decided to go on these rides in the first place? She'd be damned if she would go down without a fight.

"Let them go, Badger." It was the kid's voice. The leader whirled round, "SHUT UP, Kyle!" he snapped.

"We don't need any fucking trouble out here, Badge, just let them alone."

Marie grabbed Mona's reins and said, "Don't look back." She pulled her along as they kicked their horses into a trot. They could hear the two men arguing, the younger one trying to talk some sense into the one called "Badger."

"BITCH!" he yelled at their backs. The remark didn't surprise them but, the gunshot made Mona scream as both horses jumped, slamming into each other. They managed to stay in their saddles and calm the horses down. With white knuckles, Mona held tight to the horn and blinked back the tears pooling in her eyes. Marie glanced over her shoulder at the sound of revving motors, wondering if they would follow, but they were moving on. "Holy Mary, mother of God," she whispered to herself.

They kept the horses moving as fast as they could without pushing them too hard, until they were sure they weren't being followed. Mona was pale with fear and Marie shook in pure anger.

"I can't believe we didn't get shot back there," Mona said, after realizing they were safe.

"It was a scare tactic. Lucky for us, that Kyle kid seems to have some sense. A little later in the day and a few more shots of whiskey, and there's no telling what might have happened."

* * *

Rolex ran toward them, barking a welcome as they rode into camp on the lathered horses. Bev took one look and came marching over. "What the hell!" she said, noticing the sweat on the horses. But, when she saw the look on the riders' faces, she stopped in her tracks. "Have a run in with a bear or somethin'?" she asked.

"More like a badger," Marie replied. She had dismounted and was quickly loosening the cinches.

"A badger?"

"Yes, a man, if you could call him that. Apparently, a nickname, and it fits him well. He was with two other guys of the same caliber, and a kid about twenty. I'm going to walk these poor horses out. You explain what happened," she said to Mona.

"I ain't never had no trouble out here. Were they hunters?" Bev asked.

"These guys are not your ordinary hunters, trust me. A bunch of thugs out looking for trouble is more like it," Mona told her. The words tumbled out in a rush. Cynthia came down from the rocky hill above camp where she had been sitting in the sun. Mona again repeated the story and then listened to Bev berate them for not learning how to use a gun.

While Bev raged on, Marie removed herself to walk the horses. It was just what she needed. When her hands quit shaking and the horses were cooled off, she leaned into Ace and broke down. "You're a good boy Ace," she said, against his sweat encrusted neck. She wiped her nose against her shirt sleeve and walked the horses toward the corral.

"…I'd a shot the sons' a bitches, that's what!" Marie heard Bev bluster, when she returned.

Cynthia put her arms around Marie and then took the two leads. "I'll brush them out and put them up, honey."

"Besides, ya shouldn't go wanderin' off like that. I'm supposed to be the one takes ya out on the trails. You don't even know this country!" Bev said.

Mona looked at Marie pleadingly. She knew she should probably keep her mouth shut, but it was about to be too late for that.

"Well, Bev. If you could stay sober long enough, that might just work. So far, this has been the trip from hell, and we paid good money to have someone we could count on," Marie told her.

"Wait a damned min—" Bev said.

"No, you wait a minute! We could have been raped or even killed out there. What good would it have been to have you along, if you can't even shoot that gun you so proudly pack around? This was more serious than plugging a coyote, for God's sake!" Marie could feel the anger resurging.

Bev stood with her shoulders back, her chest puffed out like a grouse. She said nothing in defense of her behavior. Mona felt a little sorry for her. She felt bad for all of them. Marie was right; this was the trip from hell. And, it wasn't over yet.

CHAPTER 17

Cynthia busied herself with the horses, cleaning hooves and brushing out their long, silky tails. She loved talking to them; they never argued and seemed lulled into half sleep when she would hum a tune while running the soft brush over their hides.

Mona walked up to her with the dog tagging along; he rarely wandered, staying close to the horses or any humans that were willing to give him attention. Cow dogs, bred especially for being in the company of horses and moving cows, had an entirely different relationship with other ranch animals. These were referred to as 'working dogs.' But Rolex, a mixed breed, was more of a friend, always sniffing the horses' noses and staring into their faces with his head turned questioningly. It was comical and sweet at the same time. Mona smiled at Rolex and Cynthia noticed some of the stress melt away from her face.

They climbed up on the fence and sat watching the dog interact with the horses. Marie came into the corral to join them. Cynthia patted the top rail and said, "Have a seat, just be careful of splinters."

"Speaking of splinters, that woman is a pain in my butt!"

"Shhh!" Mona said. "Here she comes for round two."

"Hey, Tofu!" Bev said. She was looking right at Marie as she approached.

Marie exchanged looks with her friends, smiled, and said, "Say Bev, why do you have to be so insulting all the time?"

"I ain't. Jist can't stand spoiled, city girls is all."

"We're not spoiled, and that's really none of your business anyway. You were hired to guide us up here and, so far, you haven't kept up your end of the deal. Quite frankly, I am surprised Mrs. Frost keeps you on."

"Whadda ya expect from me?" she said mockingly.

Cynthia jumped down off the fence as Marie said, "Just do your job—sober if possible."

"In other words, Bev," Cynthia began, "'Cowboy up,' as they say out here on the range. I think that's what Marie is getting at."

"Della said you were a hell of a horsewoman. Let's just forget what has already taken place. Can we count on you to help us salvage the remainder of this pack trip?" Marie asked in a polite tone.

Bev nodded in the affirmative and shuffled her feet like a little girl. Finally, she turned and strode away without saying a word. She sulked around camp avoiding them, talking under her breath and kicking at Rolex when he came near. It bothered Cynthia, and she asked Mona if she knew whose dog Rolex was for sure: Bev's or the ranch owner's? Marie didn't know either but, Cynthia said, she planned to steal the dog when they left for home, because she couldn't stand seeing him abused.

"I thought I was the rescuer, Cyn!" Marie said.

"No, you try to save humans, which is a grave mistake. You see, animals are much more grateful."

* * *

Using Ritz Bitz crackers and Skittles candies, they played checkers on a stump that someone had carved blocks into.

"Remember that guy we played horseshoes with in Wyoming?" Cynthia asked.

"You mean the Lone Ranger?" Marie grinned at the memory. "We ate him alive, poor dude. He should have known better than to take eight women into the wilds and expect to survive."

"You were mean to him," Mona said.

"He was arrogant and needed an attitude adjustment."

"And you were the one to give it?" Mona asked. She hadn't meant to be sarcastic, and immediately felt bad; after all, Marie had just saved their skins. "I'm sorry, Marie. I guess I'm still shook up from this morning."

"It's okay, I'm a big..." She didn't finish, as everyone's attention was drawn to the sound of a helicopter. It was coming up over the ridge fast and began circling the hill tops. It slowed several times, hovering above the canyon where Mona and Marie had run into the gang of scary men.

"Think it's the police or something?" Cynthia asked.

They watched against the blinding sun as the chopper moved west of their camp. Then the noise grew louder. A few moments later, the big bird was putting down right in the middle of the swampy meadow next to their camp. Bold red letters on the side read: DEA.

CHAPTER 18

A tall man wearing black was running towards them, the helicopter's thwack so loud that Marie couldn't hear what Mona was saying as she grabbed her arm and pointed. Bev had walked forward to meet him. The horses were running in circles, tails raised as they snorted and whinnied into the air.

"DEA," he yelled over the noise, then pulled the glove from his hand reaching to shake hers. Stunned, Bev just stared at him then finally extended her hand. His black hair was tousled from the wind that the helicopter had churned up; he smiled, looking like a school boy enjoying a private joke. A few days of beard growth darkened his face, adding to his chiseled features a roguish look that any woman could appreciate.

"Just want to know if you've seen anyone up here in the past couple of days," he said.

"Yep, the girls ran across a rough bunch just this mornin'. Tried to give 'em trouble." Bev motioned for him to follow her, and they walked together toward the others.

Marie explained as quickly as she could what had happened. "Scared the hell out of us," she told him.

The agent described the man called Badger, and it was confirmed that this was the group of thugs they had seen on the trail.

"He's one bad hombre ma'am. I'd say you're damned lucky to be standing here." He smiled but his eyes wore a look of concern. Too shocked to think what may have unfolded out there this morning, Marie didn't even notice how handsome he was.

"You armed?" he asked, looking at all four women.

"I got a gun," Bev said. "But these city girls probably couldn't shoot the broad side of a barn."

"Hold on a minute, I'll be right back." He turned and sprinted back to the helicopter. Ducking beneath the chopping blades, he crawled inside. Returning a few moments later, he handed out cylinders to Marie, Mona and Cynthia. "Bear repellent. Read the directions and keep them on you at all times," he warned. Turning to Bev he said, "Pack it up and get off of this mountain first thing in the morning. All hell is going to break loose up here." Then— "What's your destination?"

"Uh, the Frost Ranch, upper Willow Forks," Bev said.

"Good. That's likely going to be our command post. Which way did you come up?"

"Riley Creek."

"Better go back through Meat Camp and pick up the trail where it circles around Wild Horse. Are you familiar with that route?"

"Well, it's rough, and we've had rain to boot."

"Take it slow. I still think you'll be safer. Those guys can't get out on four wheelers off of Wild Horse. "And," he said, "I don't want you running into them again."

Bev looked a little rattled as the man pushed a handful of what looked like dynamite into her hands. "Flares," he explained. "Anything happens, send them up. Be careful ladies," he said, nodding at Marie as if to get confirmation that they would be cautious.

She gave a nervous laugh and said, "We will."

They stood watching as the helicopter lifted with a whap, whap, whap. It circled the rocky hills for about five minutes then disappeared. They all turned to look at each other, not sure what they should do next.

"What a cutie!" Cynthia said.

"What?" Marie said, incredulous.

"He was!" she said. "Hey, this might be an ugly situation, but that was NOT an ugly man."

Mona and Marie exchanged looks of disbelief but, before they could say anything, Cynthia added, "I've always wanted to ride in a helicopter." She was staring at the sky, her hands folded across her chest.

"Oh my God!" Marie said, holding her head in her hands.

Mona was distracted by Bev who was in the corral cursing. "I'm going over to see what her problem is," she said. Bev was putting a halter on Karza, and Mona could see blood running down the horse's neck from a nasty gash. Dust still hung thick in the air from the commotion of frightened horses.

"Hey, can I help?" she offered, while opening the gate so Bev could lead the horse out.

"Cut herself on a nail or something." Bev pointed. "Gimme that red box over there."

Mona retrieved the first aid kit for horses and helped Bev doctor Karza. She offered to stitch the wound, but Bev decided that duct tape would hold it together just fine. Storming around the horse to check for more injuries, Bev was the most irritated Mona had seen yet. She wondered what was brewing in Bev's mind. Surely this injured horse wouldn't have such an effect on a woman who had probably dealt with much worse.

"Worstest pack trip I ever been on," Bev huffed in complaint.

"Me too," Mona said. She had half a mind to tell Bev that most of the trouble had been caused by her own attitude. Marie would have said so without blinking. Sometimes Mona envied Marie's blunt honesty. Mona knew it wasn't healthy to hold things inside but, for her, conflict was even worse. It always made her feel mean somehow. Still, she knew that at some point she would have to tell her friends that the rides were over for her; and that was the part she most dreaded.

CHAPTER 19

The atmosphere in camp grew tense with Bev hitting the bottle harder than ever, not even trying to hide it now. She stormed about, blurting out commands loaded with one foul word after another. Approaching Marie boldly, she put her sweaty, red face just inches from hers and said, "Git yer stuff packed an' tents down. We're leavin' in half an hour!"

"What? Are you nuts? It's getting late, and you heard that guy tell us to leave in the morning."

Bev's voice rose to an angry roar. "He ain't yer guide, and I say we get the hell out a here before them assholes show up in this camp!"

Marie shook her head. "It's too dangerous, Bev. I read about that trail, it's treacherous enough in daylight, and we would be riding in the dark." She stayed calm to avoid another explosion from Bev, speaking in a firm, but quiet tone.

"There's a full moon," Bev said, between clenched teeth.

Marie curled her nose at the smell of Bev's breath. She stared straight back at her and said, "You go then. We'll find our own way back, we don't need you." Marie was half worried that Bev might actually hit her or something, but the woman seemed speechless.

Bev closed one eye and looked over at Cynthia and Mona, trying to focus on them. There was a deadly silence before she spun around, nearly falling over. Her big, angry strides seemed comical as she tried to maneuver around the various rocks and tree limbs that littered the ground.

"Go with her if you want," Marie said, tossing her hand in the air as she walked past her two friends. But they followed her to the campfire where they all stood in silence watching their guide furiously break camp. Within minutes, she had her gear loaded on Molly and Smokey saddled. She mounted up. Riding out of camp without a word to them, Bev pulled hard on the mare's lead rope. The gelding swished his silvery tail in agitation as Bev goaded him with her boot heels.

The other horses whinnied loudly; not wanting to be separated, they paced the fence and tossed their heads as Bev rode into the trees and disappeared down the same trail they had all rode in on. Rolex stood looking at them as if he weren't sure what to do. Then they heard Bev bellow, "Come here you son of a bitch!" The dog trotted after her with his head hung to the ground. Cynthia's eyes brimmed with tears. She couldn't believe the loyalty of that dog to such an undeserving human.

The sun was quickly setting behind lingering grey clouds when Cynthia and Mona walked over to check on the horses; they were standing together in the corner of the corral looking toward the trail Bev had taken. She had left enough feed to provide the horses for the night and in the morning. Three empty whiskey bottles, one of them shattered, had been left at the spot where Bev had set up her tent. Mona bent over and began to pick up the broken pieces of glass.

"I've never seen Marie so quiet," Cynthia commented.

"This ride has about done us all in. Marie was scared and mad this morning, but she got us out of there safely. At times, she's too strong for her own good," Mona said.

"All I want—," Cynthia reached down to pick up the other

two bottles, "—is that we get out of here unscathed. Bob would be worried to death if he knew we were up here alone and in possible danger." When she stood up she felt one of those weird dizzy spells that her doctor claimed was low blood pressure. She thought it was more likely caused by last night's indulgence with the wine bottle, and their current ordeal.

They found Marie working, methodically organizing what things they could carry on their saddles, and stacking the remainder of the camping gear and other supplies in a crevice between two big rocks. She covered them with one of their tents and laid stones on the corners to keep the edges down should a wind come up.

Turning to Mona and Cynthia, Marie put her hands on her hips and informed them that they would sleep near the corral in their bags, beneath the rocky ledge. It was safer than being out in the open she insisted. She would keep watch as long as she could stay awake, then Mona would take over since she was used to night shifts and would be less likely to drift off. Cynthia offered to be awakened at dawn, saying she could saddle the horses and feed them while the others napped before heading out.

"Better to go back behind Bev. We don't have the map, but at least we are somewhat familiar with that route," Marie suggested. She felt better having a plan, and the saddles were lined up on the fence, packed and ready for tomorrow.

The women were physically and emotionally exhausted. As dusk settled in, they sought shelter together along the wall of rock. Their evening meal consisted of energy bars and grapes, they spoke only in whispers, agreeing that the important thing was to avoid Badger's bunch and arrive at the Frost ranch safely.

Marie was able to stay awake until two a.m., when Mona offered to relieve her. Several times she drifted off, only able to doze for a few minutes. Hearing distant noises that sounded like gunshots frazzled her nerves even more.

***

Next to her Cynthia stirred frequently, dreaming of murderous men in camouflage. One of them wore a pink hood over his head and, when reaching to open it, the small face of an infant surprised her. Then the baby spoke in a hissing, demonic voice, saying, "Murderer, murderer!!" Cynthia struggled to cover the face where two red eyes bored into her. Pulling frantically at the hood, she used her nails to scratch and claw as the child screamed and blood spattered on her arms.

***

"SHHH, Cyn! Quiet down," Marie whispered loudly, trying to stop Cynthia from flailing. "Are you having a nightmare?"

"Guess so," she answered. Laying her head back against the cold rock, she listened to the breeze blowing through the pines above, closed her eyes again and tried to sleep. It was no use, she couldn't shake the dream. Pulling the bag closer didn't stop the chill that enveloped her. Whenever things got stressful in her life, the dreams would return in various forms. She knew exactly what they were about: her conscience. And, why God, had she become pregnant from one indiscretion that she had regretted almost immediately? Before making the decision, Cynthia tried to convince Marie that it was something she had to do to protect Bob; he didn't deserve to be hurt in such a way. Yes, Heather had always wanted a sibling, but this was the wrong way to go about it. And Mona stayed mad for months after reminding her that she had quit the women's clinic for the very reason that she couldn't stomach the frequent abortions performed there, because babies seemed to be such an inconvenience to so many women. Cynthia understood that the pain of a failed marriage and her inability to conceive children had made Mona see things differently.

But, in the end, her friends promised her what they always had—unconditional love. Still, Cynthia had been wondering for a while about the true nature of love, and if perhaps it was conditional after all.

"Cyn?" Marie said quietly. "Cyn?"

"I hear ya," Cynthia said, resigned.

"Try to get some sleep."

Cynthia leaned into Marie's shoulder as her arm encircled her.

"Okay, mommy."

"You really are a shit Cyn, you know that?"

CHAPTER 20

The moon had moved on as a faint light crept into the eastern sky. Cynthia watched the horses begin to stir, Ace getting up from where he had been laying. She smiled as he struggled to get his big legs beneath him; she was thinking Marie's God must have a sense of humor to create animals like these, equines that could be extremely graceful in the show ring yet so comical at other times. They didn't seem to be put together for getting up and down easily. Not wanting to disturb Marie, she moved quietly as she began to gather the horses.

As she walked toward the corral, she felt a chill run through her, and reached into her jacket pocket to feel for the predator spray. At least it offered some relief. She wished Rolex were still with them. It wasn't right that those thugs out there had them feeling so vulnerable.

She divided up the feed, giving each horse a small portion of what was left. They stood patiently as she saddled them, secured the saddle bags, and put the bridles on over their halters. She left them tied and walked back to where Marie and Mona were huddled beneath the protective overhang. The sleeping bags would have to be left behind, along with almost everything else that

Molly had packed up the mountain. Marie was awake, squinting through the pines at the climbing sun while Mona yawned sleepily. Marie stashed her bag along with the other things under the tent, ordering Mona and Cynthia to do the same.

"Bossy!" Cynthia said, as she walked by. She pushed the bill of Marie's cap up, jumping to the side as Marie reached out to grab her.

They rode out in silence, except for the typical trail noises of snorting horses, jingling bridles, and the metallic sound of horseshoes against rock. Marie strained to catch the sound of motors or human voices. It angered her that Badger and his men could be on the other side of a mountain, or possibly watching from close by, and she had no way of knowing. Lack of sleep had done nothing to calm the edginess either, as she flinched at every little noise. She wished the happy little birds would just shut up so she could listen. It occurred to her that Bev may have come across Badger's bunch on her way back down to the Frost Ranch and run into trouble. Then again, maybe she was drinking whiskey with them, complaining about the three spoiled city girls she had had to leave back in camp.

An hour later they stopped for a short break, moving off the trail to seek cover beneath the trees. No one had spoken, each lost in thought and concerned for each other. It was vital to their safety to be as quiet as possible.

"This next section..." Marie said softly, "is steep and nothing but shale, remember?" Mona and Cynthia nodded. "There won't be anywhere to hide."

"Wonder if Bev got back okay?" Cynthia said.

"Who cares!" Marie retorted. "No telling what story she'll give that Frost woman."

Cynthia reached back and took two oranges and a bag of trail mix out from her saddle bags, and passed the food around.

Marie stared at the orange and said, "Max choked on an orange section once....he was three." She grew quiet. When it was peeled, she handed half of it to Mona. "I nearly ripped the shirt off my neighbor."

"What?" Mona asked, looking curiously at Cynthia.

"He was mowing his lawn. I left Max sitting on the kitchen floor, ran out and dragged the neighbor inside. 'He's choking!' I screamed as I pulled the poor man into the kitchen. Max was so terrified he spit the orange out. Scared it right out of his throat the neighbor claimed."

"Oh," Mona said as she and Cynthia exchanged glances.

Giving Ace a nudge with her heels, Marie turned back toward the trail. As Cynthia scrambled to put the trail mix away, Dino was already moving when low branches almost tore his rider from the saddle. As a result, Cynthia received a few scratches on her neck and face.

Mona hardly noticed; all she could think of was the slippery shale ahead of them. She had made up her mind to stay mounted though and trust the horse this time, using all her concentration to move with Karza's body instead of going into panic mode. The little mare picked her way carefully over the bad footing and Mona praised her in a reassuring tone: "Goood girl, Karza," she said repeatedly.

And before they knew it, they were safely off of the shale and turning onto the old logging road where it was wide and flat.

"Jeeze! Cynthia said. "That's a little unnerving on the down hill."

"Ya think?" Mona said.

Marie silently blamed herself for this disastrous ordeal. How many times did she have to remind herself that people and circumstances were out of her control; that she had spent her entire life trying to right things that had gone wrong and made very little progress? True, she was a caregiver at heart, evidenced by the profession she had chosen. And she couldn't get that Kyle kid off her mind. Her mother's heart wanted to save him, too; but her therapist mind knew that she couldn't. She felt her energy seeping away with the helplessness of it all. The one thing she could do was try to get her two best friends and herself back safely.

"What time is it?" Marie asked.

"You've got the watch," Cynthia said.

She pulled up her sleeve to check. "Ten after eight."

"Should be back by eleven or so," Cynthia commented. "Maybe Bev will have lunch waiting for us, HA!" She couldn't resist mocking Bev's own habit. Dino's head came around to shove at her stirrup in what she interpreted as approval of her joke. "I'm glad to see someone around here still has a sense of humor." She patted his long, warm neck.

When they reached the spot where Bev had shot the coyote, they rested again in the shade of the cottonwoods, this time dismounting to stretch their legs and take a quick trip into the bushes. While watering the horses at the big trough, Mona said she felt they should get a refund. Marie said they had better get one, along with an apology.

"You can't really expect that Bev has an apology in her, do you?" Mona asked.

"Della Frost has got some questions to answer, I know that much," Marie declared, as she struggled to pull the sweater over her head. It was warming up fast at this lower altitude. The sweat on Karza's neck had loosened the duct tape and the cut was oozing blood. Mona worried about it, but she would have to wait to clean and redress the wound until they got back to the ranch.

CHAPTER 21

The horses had instinctively picked up their pace as horses are known to do when they are headed towards home. Karza danced and tossed her head causing the tape on her neck to come off completely while Mona's frustration was growing by the minute. Then, suddenly her horse lunged and she almost lost her seat as Rolex came scrambling up the side of the trail. He was panting heavily as he whined and circled the riders.

Cynthia immediately dismounted and called him over to her. "What's the matter boy?" she said, as he anxiously licked at her hands and neck when she squatted next to him. "Something is wrong!" She looked up at Marie whose face showed the same concern. She gave the heated dog a drink from her water bottle and poured some of the cool liquid over his face before mounting up.

"Maybe he just came back to look for us," Mona offered. "For which he will receive another beating when we get to the barn."

"Not if I can help it!" Cynthia said.

They rode ahead cautiously, hoping whatever was going on didn't include Badger and his band of thugs. A short time later, they came around a sharp turn in the trail where it dropped off steep on one side. All three horses' heads raised, ears perking up in surprise as they came upon Molly standing in the middle of the trail, with her pack askew and leaning to one side. She turned and nickered softly, bobbing her head up and down.

Finding it hard to assess the situation, Marie began to feel panic rising inside her. Then she spotted Bev a few yards away, sitting on the side of the cliff with her legs dangling over the edge.

"Looks like Smokey dumped her ass," Cynthia said.

"Shh!" Marie warned her. "She doesn't even know we're here."

Bev looked dazed staring down over the cliff; she had a bottle of whiskey in her left hand, and the pistol lay on the ground next to her.

Mona nudged Karza up beside Marie. "Want me to try to talk to her?" she asked with an undertone of caution.

"Okay…but be careful," Marie said, reluctantly.

Mona dismounted, handed her reins to Marie and approached the guide slowly. "Bev…you all right?" she asked.

"Shmokey, stupid shuvva bish," Bev slurred. Turning to look at Mona, she lost her balance, almost falling over the edge.

"Whoa there!" Mona yelled as she reached to grab Bev's coat sleeve. That's when she caught a movement out of the corner of her eye. The big grey's mangled body was at the bottom of the ravine.

***

Cynthia sat gingerly on the sharp rocks, her tail bone already sore from days in the saddle. She held the gun in her scraped hands. They were dirty and sticky with blood from the climb down. Marie sat next to her as they looked at the poor creature, barely resembling a horse now, his skin torn, legs tangled into a grotesque pile of bone and flesh. In bizarre contrast, the horse's head didn't have a single scratch. His lips trembled over big, hay-stained teeth that were clenched over the bit in shock. An onyx eye stared at them pleadingly. Marie had to turn away.

Swallowing the sour bile that came up in her own throat, Cynthia felt like she would retch at any moment. The sun was high and the air stifling down in the rocky hole. Sweat beaded on her forehead and was dripping from her arm pits beneath her blouse. She slapped angrily at her sides with her free hand, blinking hard at tears forming against her will. She couldn't ever remember feeling so helpless. It had been years since she'd fired a gun and she had never had to put an animal down.

"Cyn?... Cyn?"

"What?" she snapped at Marie.

"We've gotta do something, he's suffering."

"What's this we shit, Marie? You take the goddamned gun then!" she said through gritted teeth while shoving it toward her friend. Her trembling hands lost their grip, and the gun tumbled noisily down into the ravine where it became wedged between two rocks.

Cynthia couldn't move. For a long time she just stared up at the sky, where she wished she could be temporarily carried away with the clouds that were moving ever so slowly across the horizon. She didn't want to be here, forced to do this thing that must be done. But in this, she had no choice – Bev was drunk and no one else knew how to use a gun.

"Are you all right?" she heard Mona's voice echo from above. She didn't answer. Taking a deep breath, she scooted down over the rocks to retrieve the weapon.

Smokey's sides were heaving beneath the ruined saddle as Cynthia reached for the gun. She started to sob when it wouldn't break free. Finally, she was able to dislodge the pistol. It felt cold and heavy as she checked to see if it was loaded. She clicked the safety off and willed her hands to stop shaking.

Cynthia held the gun with both hands, close enough to feel the hot breath blowing from his flared nostrils. Her focus was on the swirl of white hair in the middle of the horse's forehead. "I'm so sorry baby," she whispered, then pulled the trigger. The sickening thud of the bullet making contact and Smokey's big form going limp told them all they needed to know. The faint smell of gun smoke lingered in the air.

Marie made eye contact with Mona who was watching from above, her hands covering her mouth. Cynthia's head was cradled in the bend of her arm as she sat motionless for several minutes. Finally, she stood up, almost falling over on the rocks. Marie reached out to give her a hand and they began the climb back out of the rocky pit, not wanting to 'sit' with death any longer than necessary.

They left Bev where she had passed out in the shade of a tree. Mona put the gun next to her, a bottle of water and her sleeping bag. Cynthia said that maybe the coyotes would get their revenge if the woman didn't come to, soon. Mona shot her a look of disgust before offering to help Marie with Molly. While securing the pack saddle and moving items around to balance both sides, they discovered that Bev had brought along quite a cache of whiskey. It came as no surprise, but they did wonder how much Mrs. Frost knew about Bev's drinking habits. When Marie had checked out the pack station, she had been told that they were a reputable outfit and their guides some of the most experienced in Oregon. Well, this was a ride they would never forget, one that had brought a black cloud over what might have been a great experience amidst a beautiful landscape.

CHAPTER 22

"Well girls," Marie began, "I guess we better head down the trail and report to the Frost Ranch and Pack Station. Let them know their guide is passed out half way up the mountain and that they've lost a good horse because of her. And that our dear Cynthia bears the burden of having had to shoot the poor animal." Marie looked kindly at her friend," Are you alright, Cyn?"

"Yep," she said, licking the grit from her chapped lips. She could taste blood. Pulling the lip balm from the pocket of her blouse, she greased her lips liberally then put her left foot in the stirrup. A big bounce on her right foot and she climbed up on the tall red horse. Following her friends as they began their descent, Cynthia felt more tired than she could ever remember.

Mona was behind Marie, watching Ace's rump move from side to side like a plump lady in a polka-dot dress. Molly trailed behind Karza on a long lead line; she seemed to have a calming effect on the little roan. Mona wondered if they were pasture buddies.

They rode in the hot sun for over an hour never speaking to each other, when all at once they were below the tree line as the trail opened up into sage covered hills and rocky gullies that still trickled with water. They saw the ranch half a mile away and could

see a DEA helicopter sitting in the meadow by the barn. Several big
tents had been set up and numerous vehicles were parked around,
police cars and an EMT unit among them.

"Looks like Barnum and Bailey's circus!" Cynthia said, as they
pulled their horses to a stop. Rolex had been trotting behind them
with his head hung low, but when he saw the activity going on at
the ranch, he took off at a dead run, barking.

"Well, something's going on down there and I'm not so sure
I'm ready to find out what," Marie said. She took off her cap and
fanned her face with it. "Shall we ride in and find out?"

Mona just sighed and waved off a pesky fly.

Reluctantly, they moved on, taking their time until they approached the gate that led into the meadow behind the barn. Mona
got down and opened it. "Go ahead," she said, "I think I'll walk
the rest of the way." After latching the gate, she wrapped Molly's
lead around her saddle horn and fell in behind her friends, leading Karza with one rein. She had been worrying about leaving Bev
behind and wondered if they had done the right thing. If anything
happened to the woman she would never forgive herself.

Someone was riding at them on a four wheeler; as it approached, they saw that it was Mrs. Frost. She was standing up
from the seat as the machine bumped over clumps of manure and
gopher mounds. Coming to a stop, she sat down, her face wearing a questioning look. The impatient horses moved restlessly, not
wanting to stop when so close to the comforts of home.

Della killed the motor and scolded the horses. "Knock it off
you spoiled kids!" she said in a severe tone, to which they respond-
ed by quietly standing while she began to ask questions.

"Where's Bev?"

"She's passed out drunk, about an hour or so up the trail,"
Marie said.

"What's going on here?" Cynthia asked.

"Drug bust. I understand you met up with the hoodlums
yourselves! Listen, come on up to the house, Sully will tend to the

horses. I've got some questions need answering."

"No offense Mrs. Frost, but so do we," Marie said. You could have heard the proverbial pin drop even in the grassy field. After a short silence Della said, "Fair enough. I'll be in the kitchen then."

***

At the barn, they took personal belongings from their saddles and offered to help take care of the horses, but Sully wouldn't hear of it. Mona showed him Karza's injury, assuring him she had tried to keep the wound clean and covered. "Ya done jist fine, ma'am," he insisted, then he waved his hand to shoo them away, sending the women up to the house.

As they walked along the driveway, they were approached by a smiling, blond-haired woman wearing a business suit and tottering on high heels. "Here we go," Marie said under her breath.

"Hello ladies. My name is Nancy and I'm with KT..."

Della's warning voice came from the back porch where she stood with her hands on her hips. "Don't talk to her!"

"Dammit!" the woman said before she strode off, scowling. Cynthia giggled when "Nancy" nearly stepped in a pile of fresh manure. She turned to give them a dirty look before she retreated toward her SUV, where another reporter, a man, was bent over laughing.

They dropped their bags on the steps and followed Della into the house, where they all took a seat around the small kitchen table. The first thing out of her mouth was, "Where's Smokey?"

Marie cleared her throat indicating she would answer the question, for which her two friends looked most grateful. "There... was an accident, Mrs. Frost," Marie started.

"I wish you'd call me Della, please."

"Della. Smokey fell...we had no choice. You see, we had to... put him down. Cynthia did since she knew how...to use a gun, that is."

The anger melted from her face and was replaced with a deep

sadness. She paused for a long time, blotted her eyes with a napkin from the pile on the table and then swallowed hard.

"I am sorry for being so short with you, what with all these government people taking over my ranch and me finding out why my cattle have been disappearing and that boy getting shot, I am just..."

"What boy?" Marie asked.

"Oh, he's a local kid, not really a boy anymore, but he was runnin' with that bunch I guess. He used to go to school down in Willow Forks and was a good little football player. We had high hopes for him goin' places with it."

"Kyle," Marie said.

"Yes. Kyle Delaney. One of the gang members shot him in the back as he was giving himself up. They air lifted him out last night. I haven't heard if he's gonna make it. I still can't believe he got tangled up with Badger—although Kyle's mother used to be his girlfriend. That man was no damned good I can tell you. He's been in and out of jail, even raped a woman over in Idaho and walked off scot-free. However, he won't be causing any more misery 'round this country."

"So, they've got him in custody?" Mona asked.

"Nope. Shot and killed him dead is what I heard."

They all looked at each other in shock. Della then changed the subject, saying that Bev had let her down once again. She admitted that Sully had voiced concern that Bev was sneaking booze but she just didn't believe him. "I thought she had pulled her head out of the trough, guess I was wrong," she confessed.

They told her about Bev's behavior and how she had burned her hand. Mona related that she had tried to befriend her and seemed to make some progress but, when Bev drank, there was no reasoning with the woman.

"Oh, I know. You don't have to tell me. I've had to send her away more than once."

"Then why on earth did you trust her to take us out?" Marie asked.

"Like I said, I thought my niece had pulled in the reins and was in control."

"Your niece?" This was the first time Cynthia had spoken since they had entered the house.

"Well, Charlie's niece. My husband's name was Charlie."

The woman swore that Bev had taken several groups of hunters out in the fall, all of them men. They were very happy with her guiding, she said.

"She doesn't seem to like women much, that's for sure," Mona commented.

"She accused us of being lesbians, which was really annoying," Marie said.

"Bev has never been close with women. I guess I'm probably the only woman she's come near to trusting. She doesn't understand friendships like you three have. Now, I'm not making excuses for her by any means, but I think there are some things I should tell you about our Beverly."

CHAPTER 23

"Charlie and his sister, Gayle, were raised outside of Modesto, California on a cattle ranch. Gayle was spoiled by her father and was never made to work. In spite of that, she resented Charlie. Shoulda been the other way around if you ask me." Della smiled. "Well, the ranchers and farmers were getting crowded out and Charlie's folks were getting older so they sold out to developers. That's when Charlie, as a young man, came up to Oregon where he worked on ranches all over the valley as a buckaroo. We met at a brandin' and…you don't need to hear all this," she said.

"Go on," Cynthia said.

"Yes, go on. We want to hear it," Marie added.

"Well, to shorten it up, Gayle was a mess living down there in the city. After her folks died and there was no one to keep carrying her financially, she started moving in with one man after another and ended up with a baby—Beverly. By then Gayle was drinking and hitting the bars, leaving Bev with anyone who would watch her. There were men in and out of the house who abused her." Della looked down at the table solemnly. "We found out later that Beverly had also been molested."

"Oh Della, I'm sorry," Mona said.

"We were childless, Charlie and I. We started going down to California in the summers and bringing Beverly up here to spend time on the ranch. She thrived here and got to be quite a little cowgirl. We tried to talk her mother into letting Bev come up and go to school, stay with us, but she would never agree to it. We even asked to adopt her and Gayle got so mad she didn't let her come up that year. She'd have lost the welfare money she had become accustomed to, which is why I think she refused. And, no doubt, to also spite Charlie." Della got up and started making coffee as she continued her story.

"Beverly's agriculture teacher told her about a job at a pack station in the Sierras and, on the day she turned eighteen, she hitchhiked up there and took the job. That's where she met Jimmy." Della's eyes sparkled when she looked at them. "Now, you can see for yourself Bev is no beauty but, Jimmy, he loved her so. Said he had found his 'angel in the rough.' They worked together for two years and then Bev ended up pregnant. They had two of the most beautiful children you ever laid eyes on.

"First, Jim junior was born, and a year later a little girl they named Angela. We begged them to move up here so we could help them and, of course, to be around the children." She winked at them and sat the coffee pot on the table along with four cups, then sat down again.

Della sipped her coffee, took a deep breath and exhaled. "There was a flood you see. They were all in the truck, the two children strapped into their car seats in the extra cab. From what witnesses said, Jimmy got out at a bridge to check if it was safe to cross. He was swept away by a wall of water. Bev must have panicked. She tried to go across with the truck and it got stuck.

"A man who came on the scene said the truck was filling with water, and Bev was frantically trying to free her babies from those seats when the truck broke loose and was washed down river. The man saved Beverly's life, but he said she fought him the whole time. They found Jimmy's body and the babies, still in their seats.

It was the saddest funeral you can imagine. We never saw Beverly cry, not once. And she don't ever talk about it. I think she wanted to go with them." Della got up and started wiping the counters and moving about the kitchen.

"My God, that's awful," Mona said. Cynthia was wiping her eyes, her dirty hands leaving dark smudges on her face. Marie was quiet, brushing imaginary crumbs from the table. "That explains a lot about Bev's behavior," she finally said.

There were male voices drifting in from the porch, and they could see through the window that Sully was talking to the same agent that had landed in their camp yesterday.

"Ma'am?" Sully said, peeking through the slightly open door.

"Bring 'em in Sully. Might as well make a party out of all this, I reckon."

The agent pushed his sun glasses up onto his head as Sully led him and what looked like an undercover officer, into the kitchen. Marie immediately felt a tingling sensation all over her body. She wondered if he had this effect on all women. Everyone shook hands and introductions were made as Marie floated off in thought while conversation was being carried on all around her.

"Did you hear me gal?" Della was asking.

"What? No," Marie said. "I'm sorry, I'm just so…"

"I said, you ladies can stay upstairs in the spare room; take a shower and get some rest. Then these gentlemen would like to ask you a few questions. We'll all meet down here in my living room in a couple of hours, if that suits you." Della looked around.

"Sure…yah…ok," came the replies as they got up, chair legs scraping loudly on the wood floor.

"You won't get any cell service here ladies, so feel free to use the phone in the kitchen to call your men or whatever," Della offered.

"I don't have a man," Marie spit out with immediate regret. A look at the agent and she blushed red. With eyebrows raised, he flashed her a mischievous grin.

CHAPTER 24

From the window upstairs they could see the place was swarming with officials of one kind or another, some talking on radios whose scratchy nasal calls drifted out over the ranch. Mona and Marie were not looking forward to the questioning. Exhausted, all they could think about was getting back home and away from the disappointment this trip had caused each of them.

"I guess they won't have any interest in talking to me, I never laid eyes on those skinheads or whatever they were," Cynthia said, from the bathroom.

"You are not getting out of this, sister!" Marie said. "It should be entertaining at the very least."

"I'll be there. I wanna see that hunk from the helicopter." She laughed as she turned on the shower.

"Oh, brother!" Mona said, shaking her head.

Della knocked at the door and, as Marie opened it, she handed her a tray containing sliced cheese, meat, crackers and little red boxes of raisins. "Don't know what happens to my manners sometimes, you must be starving. This should keep you alive until you're ready to come down." They thanked her, and she told them there would be elk stew on the stove whenever they felt like a real meal.

After a hot shower Cynthia called home. Bob was out, so she told Heather that the trail ride had ended early because of a couple of incidents that she would tell them about when she got back. She then fell asleep sprawled out on the double bed. Marie claimed the top part of the day bed near the window where a fan was pulling the cool air in off of the grassy yard below. Mona waited to take an extra long shower in an attempt to melt away the tension in her mind and body. Then she tried to rest on the bottom section of the bed upon which Marie was now snoring. She eventually gave up and sat in an old wing-backed chair to read.

I should be tired, she kept telling herself while thumbing through a cattlemen's magazine. Reading about everything from artificial insemination to ranchers going belly up because of environmentalists, she finally dropped it on the night stand and headed downstairs.

As soon as she opened the door, the aroma of the stew caused her mouth to water. She became distracted though when she stopped to look at some of the photos lining the walls of the stairwell. Many were old black and whites, having become yellowed by the years. There were pictures of the ranch and numerous shots of men on horseback or driving teams that pulled plows and hay wagons. Other photos were of more gentlemanly types posed along a town boardwalk; they were dressed in vests and hats and held smoking cigars. To Mona they looked arrogant standing next to their dour-faced women in cumbersome clothing, impractical for such hard life on the land.

"Men, pshh!" she muttered. Then a brass framed picture of a little girl caught her eye. It was in color and, although the child was plain, long golden braids reached to her lap as she sat in an oversized saddle smiling down at the camera. Mona recognized it as Bev and was suddenly overcome with an unusual sadness, reminding herself that they had all been children once. Some wounded more than others, but all of them dragged along by the adults who made the decisions in their lives. They were always forced to accept whatever circumstances they found themselves in. Emergency rooms were full of these unfortunate children, this she knew all too well.

Della had set out bowls on the counter and a pan of biscuits, along with a note saying there were sodas in the refrigerator and insisting that they make themselves 'at home.'

The kitchen was bright with the midday sun pouring in through the wood-framed windows, where blue, checkered curtains had been pulled to the side. Mona basked in the quaintness of her simple surroundings, black cast iron skillets hanging from hooks above the stove, crocheted pot holders, and an ancient chrome toaster sitting on the green Formica counter top.

She could live like this, she believed. Give up a high paying, high stress job and move to the country. Find a small town where she could work in a local clinic. Why not? She didn't have any family except for her sister in Florida, whom she saw only once a year if they were lucky. It occurred to her that singleness did have its advantages, if it weren't for the constant loneliness.

Feet stomped on the back porch, and Mona was jolted out of her private thoughts. "I think it would have done her some good to walk off that mountain..." Della was saying. She stopped talking to Sully when she saw Mona at the table. "Our local sheriff's posse is on the way. Gonna go up and fetch Bev," she said to Mona, as if it were a regular occurrence.

Sully took his hat off and hung it up among all the other caps, bridles and coats. "Aw, it sure smells good in here ma'am," he said as he dished out a big helping of stew and sat down across from Mona. Bowing his head, he said a silent prayer then crumbled two biscuits on top of his food. Mona finished the small portion she had in her bowl before smearing homemade huckleberry jam on half of a biscuit as she watched Sully polish off the huge bowl of stew. She wondered where such a small man could put so much food, wishing she could eat like that and not have to worry about gaining weight.

The stew was wonderful; she was thinking about a second helping when the phone rang. Della got up to answer it, but quickly motioned for Mona to take the call. It was Bob wondering what was going on, and if Cynthia was feeling all right. He asked if he should drive over.

"I don't see any reason for that Bob. Marie and Cyn are napping; we plan to leave as soon as these law enforcement people talk to us. It will probably be early tomorrow morning. We're okay, really. And we'll tell you all about this ordeal when we get back to Salem."

"I'm worried about her Mona," he said, sounding tired. "Doctor Blake has called twice, says he needs to meet with us in his office. He won't tell me anything…privacy issues I guess."

"That's normal physician's protocol, Bob. I wouldn't worry too much."

***

"What is going on with Dr. Blake, Cyn?" Mona asked her friend as she stomped into the room. Cynthia was putting her socks on and looked up at Mona with annoyance.

"Well, I didn't want it getting out but…we're having an affair." She smiled coyly at Mona then said in a matter-of-fact tone, "He did some tests because of this dizziness is all. What's got you all riled up?"

"Bob called and he is worried about you, that's what! Is this going to be like before when…?" Mona saw Marie sit up quickly.

"Mona!" Marie said, with a brittle edge to her voice. "Look, we've all been through a lot the past couple of days, but there is no need to take it out on one another!"

Mona held the small glass door knob in her hand, her knuckles white as she focused on the old black key hole and tried to calm herself. Suddenly, she turned to Cynthia and said, "You don't even know how lucky you are."

Slamming the door behind her, she took the stairs two at a

time in an effort to run away from the scene she had just created. She couldn't let go of what Cynthia had done and knew she had simply sought revenge when she had betrayed her to Heather. It was eating at her and she had built a wall of anger to keep Cynthia away.

In the kitchen, Mona told Della she was going down to the barn to check on Karza. When she opened the door, Rolex greeted her with a lick to her extended fingers. "C'mon big boy," she said, as he walked alongside her.

The company of the dog was a balm for the pain she was feeling. No—guilt—masked by her own feelings of superiority for being the good person that she thought she was; it made her feel sick.

She had wanted marriage and children, the very things Cynthia had taken for granted. Mona was inwardly jealous and knew it as a demon she should slay, but how? Oh God, how? Was it too late? She hadn't actually told Heather about the incident in Mexico or the abortion, the girl had guessed most of the details. The truth was, Mona had betrayed her dear friend to her own daughter and there were no excuses in the universe valid enough for what she had done. This she knew for a certainty.

Karza's soft muzzle was cupped in her hands and she could feel the warmth of the mare's breath, smell the 'horsey' scent she had come to enjoy so much. It was the love of horses that had bonded this trio of friends: was there some magic in it that could heal the wounds that festered between them?

Mona walked back towards the house, determined to salvage what she could of the friendship she had spent the past decade building, with two of the strongest, most loving women she would ever know. A truck pulling a trailer full of already saddled horses rattled past her on the dirt drive.

CHAPTER 25

"Marie?" Cynthia stood at the bathroom mirror brushing her hair.

"Huh?"

"I do know how lucky I am," she said.

"I know you do." Marie stepped inside and picked hairs from the back of Cynthia's sweat shirt. "I'm starving, let's go down and eat."

Just then the rattle of metal and whinny of horses drew their curiosity to the window. An older, white stock trailer with a faded gold star pulled by a beat up old pick-up was headed down to the barn. They could barely make out the words 'Sheriff Posse' painted on the trailer's side.

"Think they might be going up to get Bev?" Cynthia asked.

"I wouldn't doubt it," Marie said, shrugging her shoulders.

"I feel kinda bad, don't you?"

"Not really. C'mon." Marie's answer was curt as she pulled her friend away from the window.

Della seemed to have been waiting for them in the kitchen, and quickly ladled out generous portions of stew into bowls then retrieved coleslaw from the refrigerator. Sitting down across from

Marie, Della wore a faint smile and there was a kind of twinkle in her eyes when Marie glanced up from her bowl. When she looked at the ranch woman a second time, Della was sitting back in her chair with her arms folded across her chest. Marie stirred a mushy potato around and cut a carrot into bite size pieces, sensing that Della had something on her mind.

"Is there anything you want to tell me?" she asked, glancing at Cynthia to see if she had noticed the woman's odd behavior. Cynthia looked from one to the other and went back to eating.

"I guess I'll need to tell you, since you ain't noticed," she answered.

"Noticed what?"

"That helicopter man has been asking a lot of questions about you. Why, he's got you in his cross hairs, gal!" she said, leaning forward across the table for emphasis.

Cynthia burst out laughing, reaching for a napkin to wipe the food from her chin. "Mrs. Frost, Marie doesn't notice when men have the hots for her," Cynthia offered.

Marie gave Cynthia a hard look just as the back door opened and Rolex came bounding into the kitchen with Mona behind him. He circled the table, greeting each of them before taking a long drink from his bowl of water in the corner. The dog then picked up the dish next to it in his teeth and brought it to Della, where he deposited it at her feet and stood back cocking his head to the side comically. When he nosed the dish closer to Della, Cynthia squealed with delight at the dog's antics. "He's sooo cute!" she said, deliberately avoiding eye contact with Marie.

"You can't have my stew, Rolex, I don't care how much you show off," Della scolded, then, she got up and scooped kibbles from a bag of dog food and put it in front of him. He had a definite look of disappointment as he lay down with the bowl between his front paws and stared up at her. Eventually he gave in, crunching noisily at the food while scooting the bowl along the floor.

"Whose dog is he, by the way?" Cynthia asked.

"Well, my niece brought him up here two years ago from California, but he's taken to me, unless of course the horses go out. Then he wants to follow along. Which reminds me—I gotta go down and talk to the posse before they head out. They're goin' to get Beverly." Before anyone could say a word, she jumped up and was out the door.

The glow of sundown lit the country kitchen with a golden light as Marie, Mona and Cynthia began cleaning up. Cynthia was sweeping the floor and teasing Rolex with the broom when Mona asked, "They will be riding down in the dark, won't they?"

"It sorta looks like it," Marie said with an exaggerated country drawl, as she cleared the table. Mona had her hands in warm soapy dishwater while watching out of the window above the kitchen sink.

Outside, Sully was on a backhoe digging a hole, scooping one bucket of dirt at a time. As he swung around, the bucket tilted up like the head of some great beast throwing up its dinner onto the ground. They learned later that it was to be Smokey's grave, and that the DEA agent had somehow arranged to air lift the horse back to the ranch to be buried. Della told them that this information was, "…just between you and me and the fence post," to which Cynthia said, "Scout's honor, mum's the word."

Within half an hour of finishing the clean up and climbing the stairs, they were summoned downstairs again to answer questions and exchange contact information with the four men who waited in the ranch office. To their surprise, the questioning was brief, taking less than an hour. There was an official from ATF, the local State Police, the County Sheriff, who seemed very subdued, and the ever-smiling and handsome DEA agent, who had visited them in camp the day before.

His eyes were frequently scoping out Marie, which made her ponder Della's earlier observation. She felt stupidly giddy and annoyed at the same time. Aside from that irritation, there was one thing that she needed to know. Clearing her throat she said, "I have a question. The young man who was shot…is he going to live?"

The sheriff answered, "Kyle is in surgery, as we speak. The bullet entered under the left shoulder. There are some bone fragments that have to be removed, but otherwise he's doing fine." It was evident from his somber expression that he was genuinely concerned about Kyle.

Relieved, Marie still worried what kind of charges the kid would face when it was all over.

They were all feeling tired when the men left the house and Sully entered, dirty and exhausted. Della told him he was the one she needed most and to hell with all these 'cops.' She wasn't exactly thrilled that they were doing their business camped out on her land anyway. After all, it hadn't been them, but a rancher eight miles away who had alerted her when he had discovered a pack of hungry coyotes dragging a steer's hide around with the Frost Ranch brand.

It was then that she realized why cattle were disappearing from her allotment at about two per month. She figured it had to be poachers and someone who was sticking around the area. Until this morning, she had no idea a group of skinheads had holed up in caves just miles away, had stockpiled illegal firearms, ammunition, dynamite and drugs, to wait out the inability of the government to keep order in America. It seemed ludicrous and yet she had heard of these 'crazies' in the news. It was just surprising to imagine them in her little part of the world where everything seemed quiet and relatively safe.

When the sheriff's posse returned around midnight, voices drifted up from the barn along with the familiar clang of metal trailer doors, snorting horses and engines rumbling, as they made their way up past the house. Marie listened in the dark, wondering if Bev had been brought in safe. This was one of the most unreal situations she could ever remember, and yet something seemed to be happening that all of them needed to pay attention to.

Mona slept solidly until four a.m., when the cold high desert air crept into the room, waking her. She got up and removed the fan from the window, closing it quietly. After a long attempt to go back to sleep, she gave up.

Eventually hearing noises downstairs, she dressed and headed for the kitchen where the coffee was on and bacon sizzled in a pan on the stove top. Della was moving about the room on automatic pilot it seemed, and Sully sat at the table with a soiled and tattered Bible in front of him, his head lowered as he peered through a big magnifying glass.

CHAPTER 26

"Mishh Della, did you ever hear about the rich cowboy, way back in Bible times, who lived in a tent?" Sully asked.

"Nope," she said, turning bacon with a long metal fork.

"Says right here in Genesis, '…and Abram went up out of Egypt, he, and his wife, and all that he had…and Abram was very rich in cattle, in silver and in gold.'"

"Ain't seen much silver, and never any gold, Sully, unless you count my wedding ring. But this old cowgirl has spent many a night in cow camp freezing her butt off in a danged ol' tent… as you well know."

Mona heard all this in the hallway before entering the kitchen.

"Mornin'," Della said, as Mona helped herself to a cup of coffee. "Them other two stirrin' yet?" she asked. Sully acknowledged Mona with a bob of his balding head and closed the Bible, pushing it to the side. He meticulously wrapped the magnifying glass in a piece of soft deer hide, tying it with string and placed it on top of his Bible. A stack of plates with silverware on top was in the center of the table. From the warm oven, Della retrieved a platter piled high with bacon, a large bowl of fried potatoes and another of scrambled eggs. The toaster popped out two slices of nearly burned bread which she buttered and added to the tower of toast stacked on a small plate.

"There," she said, turning to open the refrigerator. Her braid swung like a heavy rope as she began grabbing ketchup, jams and jellies, milk, Tabasco sauce and a jar of homemade applesauce. Mona watched Sully in disbelief as he managed to make use of almost every kind of condiment on the table. He shook Tabasco sauce onto his eggs and squeezed ketchup on his potatoes. Then he jellied his toast, added a slice of bacon and folded it in half before dipping it in his milk and stuffing nearly the whole thing in his mouth.

Noticing Mona's astonishment, Della said, "Watching Sully eat ain't much different than slopping hogs!"

"I see that," Mona said, smiling. He stopped chewing for a few seconds then went on to attack the rest of his breakfast as if it were his last meal on earth. Mona was thinking to herself that the ease which country life brought to these people was something definitely to be envied.

When she finished eating, she thanked Della and poured two cups of coffee, balancing them carefully as she made her way up the steep steps with one in each hand.

Cynthia was curled up in a blanket looking out the window. "Goodie!" she said when Mona handed her the cup. "Marie's in the shower."

Mona opened the door, steam wafting out into the room. Over the shower noise, she yelled, "Here's a cup of Jo for you, Marie."

"Thanks!" she said, as Mona set it on the vanity.

Closing the door, Mona turned just in time to see Cynthia grabbing onto a chair as she struggled to stand up. She looked dizzy.

"Whew," Cynthia said, while Mona pretended she hadn't noticed. She was relieved that they would soon be home and Bob could get Cyn to the doctor.

By 7:30 a.m., they had tidied the room, were packed and down in the kitchen saying their goodbyes. Cynthia grabbed a slice of bacon and a piece of toast, Marie just wanted another cup of coffee and a small helping of eggs, even though Della insisted they would surely die if they didn't eat more.

"I need to see you in my office for a minute please," she said as she walked from the kitchen. The three looked at each other and followed with duffle bags in tow. Rolex was stretched out on an old sheep hide in front of Della's desk. He peeked through slits in his eyes, barely acknowledging them until Cynthia bent to pet him.

The ranch woman handed Marie an envelope across the desk. "I'm refunding your money, and want to apologize once again for all you had to endure over the past few days."

It was quiet in the room. Della walked around and approached Cynthia. Resting her hands on both of Cynthia's shoulders, she looked her in the eyes and said, "I'm sorry it fell on you to have to end my poor Smokey's suffering. I know how hard that can be. You're a brave little lady, in my estimation."

And in the weeks that followed, both Mona and Marie would reflect on those words many times.

***

The green of the west slope always made Marie feel at home even though home to her was now Portland. She missed Salem, her friends, and the quaint little neighborhood where she and Max had lived. Her heart held a mixture of countless sweet memories from both cities, darkened by one black moment on the morning when she had learned of her son's death. She forced a deep sigh to purge those thoughts and tried to focus on something positive.

It was good that they had taken the time this morning to stop so that Cynthia could see that bear. And Mona's fears were eased when the man who cared for the animal explained that he had been rescued and so could never survive in the wild. Indeed, the big creature seemed very content wrestling playfully with his owner while accepting raw carrots and dog treats. Cynthia couldn't stop talking about how beautiful the bear was, and it seemed to take everything she had to keep her from going into the big enclosure to snuggle with him.

"Holy crap!" Cynthia said when she spotted the huge piles of bear dung. Mona was embarrassed as everyone started laughing, except for a pair of traveling bicyclists; they straddled their bikes, arms folded, and obviously were not happy about a 'caged' bear. A few minutes later, the couple pulled their helmets on and pedaled off angrily.

Mona thanked the man for introducing 'Ephraim,' to them, before Marie insisted that they had to get on the road. She pried Cynthia from the chain-link fence and said, "We've got to get going, Cyn!"

***

As she drove off the I-5 coming into Salem, Marie was trying to remember a comment Della had made. The woman said she had decided that they were the 'three C's,' which she claimed meant they each had a role in their friendship. "I see you as the Commander," she told Marie. To which Marie commented that she had been accused of that before.

"And what is Cyn?" Marie asked.

"The Comedian, of course!"

"That makes sense. And Mona?" Marie wanted to know.

"Mona is the Comforter, I believe."

"Complainer is more like it lately," Marie said with a laugh.

As she pulled into Cynthia's driveway, Bob was mowing the lawn and didn't notice them, until Heather, who had pulled the living room curtains aside, came running out to the jeep to greet them.

Two weeks later Marie would be back in Salem with a big, stuffed brown bear sitting next to her on the passenger seat. She had talked to the thing all the way down from Portland, even punching him a few times when he refused to tell her why life was so damned unfair.

CHAPTER 27

From the Sinclair's back porch, Bob and Mona watched in silence as Cynthia walked toward the fence that separated their property from the neighbors and half a dozen milk goats. Cynthia had spoiled the goats with slices of apple and treats from the local feed store.

"I'm going to have to add another strand of wire to the top of that fence or those nanny goats will be coming over into my garden soon," Bob said.

"She loves those unruly goats," Mona offered, with no emotion in her voice.

The late day's sun was a golden haze, suspended over the valley in a stillness that did not invite speech. Cynthia's soft laughter floated up to the house as the goats stood on the fence competing for goodies and attention. A sparrow landed on the metal railing close to Mona, peering at her with one bright eye and turning its head to the side. Mona didn't want to move or breathe, afraid it would fly off. She had never been so close to a wild bird before. Noticing the delicate little feet and how they gripped the railing perfectly, she was amazed at the details of this unexpected visitor. The soft grey feathers of its chest beckoned her to touch them but, as she moved her hand slowly toward the bird, it hopped away along the rail with tail up, opened its beak and flew away.

Mona was waiting for Bob to speak first when he cleared his throat and said, "It's an inoperable tumor in her brain." He was swirling his iced tea around in the glass and watching as Cynthia walked back toward the house. Motionless in her chair, Mona asked the question that she already knew the answer to, "Cancer?"

"Yes," he said, in a voice cracking with grief.

***

As she wandered through the shops in downtown Portland, Marie wasn't sure why she was there. All she knew was that it felt better being among strangers that had no idea how heavy her heart was at the moment than with her colleagues from work. She even smiled at an old man who had opened the door for her. But when a woman behind the counter at the health food co-op asked her if she could help her find anything, she wanted to say, "Sure, you don't happen to have a cure for cancer lying around somewhere, do you?" Instead she bought some cleansing tea and a bar of goat milk soap.

Later, in front of a toy store, Marie thought about Max. Why not take on two doses of pain, she was thinking as she went inside. This was no regular toy store, it was a children's paradise filled with unique toys, educational games and devices Marie had no idea even existed.

In one aisle a hippy-type woman wearing a long denim skirt sat on the floor nursing her infant, while two other children lay on their stomachs enthralled with a copy of the 'Ugly Duckling', complete with quacking noises. Stepping over them, Marie rounded the corner to the stuffed toy section where the shelves against the wall were filled floor to ceiling, Max's favorites had been stuffed toys when he was little and she knew it was probably because she would never let him have a dog. Hey, she thought, the two of them lived in apartments with no yards—not fair to a dog! She let him have a cat once which was hit by a car. Max was so heartbroken over it that she had said 'no' to any more animals.

Max had never taken an interest in the horses she so loved to spend time with, and she couldn't hold it against him. Horses weren't for everyone. On one occasion they had debated over whether one could 'cuddle' with a horse. Max claimed he had won when he said that it would have to be a miniature equine, small enough to fit in his bed and ride in the front seat of the Jeep before it could be a 'real' companion in his opinion.

"Oh Max," she said softly through brimming tears. And then Marie spotted it, a huge stuffed bear, custom made for Cynthia. He was way up high and she looked around for someone to help get him down.

CHAPTER 28

There was a car Marie didn't recognize, sitting along the curb where she usually parked in front of Bob and Cynthia's, and the driveway was blocked by Mona's truck. Irritated, Marie whipped around and pulled up in front of a house across the street. Grabbing only her purse, she locked the car and walked over to the Sinclair home. Marie had to ring the bell twice before Heather came to the door. When Marie hugged her, the girl didn't respond and averted her eyes, turning back toward the dining room where someone was talking quietly.

Marie followed Heather to the table where Mona sat next to a middle-aged, African-American woman dressed in a nurse's uniform; they were looking over a stack of papers and didn't seem to know she was there. Marie went to Cynthia and bent down to hug her. She was unprepared for what she saw: Cyn, gaunt with black circles around her eyes that made her appear much older than she was. And it had happened in just a matter of weeks! Why hadn't Mona warned her? When Bob nodded at Marie, his expression exuded pain.

"Hello, I'm Dawn and you must be a friend," the nurse said. She had one of the kindest voices Marie had ever heard. Extending her hand, the nurse smiled in such a genuine way it caught Marie off guard. Then she took Marie's hand in both of hers with a profound gentleness that brought tears to her eyes.

Marie turned to look for Heather and saw that she was in the kitchen, sitting at the counter. When Marie went to her, she was doodling with a marker on the cover of a woman's fashion magazine. Marie put her hand on Heather's shoulder but the teenager squirmed away. Without saying a word, she capped the pen, slid off the stool and shuffled down the hall. A moment later, Marie heard the door to Heather's bedroom shut softly.

***

"What do you mean there is nothing that can be done? There has got to be something!" Marie leaned against her car, talking with Mona; inside she was screaming with frustration.

"The only thing doctors have suggested is radiation to…"

"To kill the cancer, right, so she can get better?" Marie asked.

"It might shrink the tumor enough to take pressure off the brain." Mona sighed. "You saw her Marie. We've got to accept that we're losing her."

"I don't have to accept shit," Marie said, her face distorted with emotion. "Don't tell me what I have to accept, Mona!" As Marie raised her voice, a man a few houses down looked up from his flower bed where he knelt.

They stood on the sidewalk, glaring at each other, the bright sun overhead mocking the darkness of the moment. Mona finally broke the silence. "Heather is hurting, she's closing down."

"I noticed."

"I'm worried. Maybe you can help?" Mona suggested.

"She doesn't need a therapist right now, she needs a friend. You've always been close to her. Try to get her out of the house and doing things with her peers. Kids are good for each other at times like this."

"Nice car by the way," Mona said. Cupping her hands around

her eyes, she peered through the tinted window. "Is that…a bear?"

"Yeah." Marie looked away. "I feel kinda stoopid about it now. I mean, what was I thinking? Like a stuffed bear is going to…" She rambled nervously, her New York accent suddenly pronounced.

Mona grabbed her hand and looked at her friend. "She'll love it, Marie," she said.

***

Seated in her car, Marie looked around at the interior of the new Porsche she had purchased on a whim last week. How frivolous, she thought. Between that and the smell of a half-eaten egg McMuffin from that morning, she felt sick to her stomach. Dialing her office in Portland, she informed her secretary that she would be back on Wednesday instead of Monday. "I need a couple of days with Cyn, she's worse than I expected."

"I'm so sorry Marie. Take your time, we'll handle things here."

"Thanks Jen." The call ended. Leaning back against the head rest, she closed her eyes. There was so much she wanted to tell Cynthia. She wondered what she could do to help. Did they even need or want her here right now? She felt a little stab of pain at having been left out of whatever discussion was going on when she intruded that morning. Mona would be the one needed now. Since Marie had moved to Portland to climb the ladder of success, she had felt herself more on the fringes than in the 'loop' of their friendship.

Bob insisted she could stay with them, but she begged off and got a room at a nearby Best Western instead. After unloading her bags, Marie turned on the television, keeping the volume low, and grabbed the pillows from the other bed. She stretched out on her bed and instantly fell asleep.

The sun had set when Marie woke up, not remembering at first where she was. She went to the double sink counter and dug out face wipes from her make-up bag, wiping the smeared mascara from beneath her puffy eyes. Running a brush through her hair, she stood in front of the huge mirror that covered the whole wall. They were all going to have dinner together tonight, she, Mona and the Sinclairs, including Bob's sister from California. It was sure to be awkward and Marie wondered if it was even a good idea. It was always Cyn who kept everyone laughing, Cyn who loved to cook and entertain.

Marie left the room and got into her car, knowing she had to make every minute with Cynthia count. She looked up at the darkening sky: rain.

CHAPTER 29

Bob barbequed chicken and Cynthia made her famous Texas coleslaw. There was a lot of laughter that evening, especially when the three women related the details of their recent trail ride in Eastern Oregon. Bob's sister, Julia, said she would have been terrified, and she didn't know how Cyn had mustered the strength to shoot a suffering animal. "I can't even step on a bug," she told them. She was as sweet-natured as her brother and doted over Cynthia constantly. Even Heather seemed to come out of her shell, teasing her mom about trying to be 'Annie Oakley.'

Marie noticed that the family dog, Tobe, had been hanging out in the house. The shaggy old sheep dog had always been kept in the backyard, where his custom-built house even had a heat lamp in the winter. He was staying close to Cyn as if he were there to comfort her in some way her human companions could not.

While doing the dishes with Mona, Marie brought up the question of animals comforting humans. Mona said the hospice nurse had encouraged it. "You just let that ole dog soothe her soul. It's amazing what animal love can do for the sick," she had told Cyn's family. Hospice: this was the first time anyone had mouthed those words. Marie left the sink, her hands dripping with soapy water as she sought the privacy of the bathroom.

***

On Wednesday morning, Marie drove out of Salem, heading north on Interstate 5 and into Portland. She went straight to the office without stopping first at her apartment. After grabbing a yogurt from the staff room refrigerator and a cup of hot coffee, she sat down at her desk to check e-mails. Her office assistant came into the room with a slight grin on her face, put both hands down on Marie's desk as she leaned forward and said, "Have you been keeping someone a secret?" Her eyebrows were raised.

"Jenny, quit with the cuteness and just spit it out, okay?"

"Drew Parish?"

"Drew....what?" Marie was annoyed, but the name was ringing a mental bell.

"What a hunk! Where did you meet him? You never go anywhere except down to that horse farm where you keep that Duke boarded," she said.

"Oh my God!" Marie suddenly remembered. "That D.E.A guy. He came here to the office?"

"Yep, left two voice mails, too," she said with a smile. "Better call him back, sounded important." Chuckling, she left the room.

A few minutes before quitting time Marie finally picked up the phone to dial the cell number Mr. Parish had left on her voice mail. She vacillated between curiosity about what he wanted and an outright attraction to the man, whom, she had assumed, she would never set eyes on again after leaving the Frost Ranch. She didn't leave a message when the cell's electronic voice mail kicked in. The other number he had left was a home phone with an area code she recognized as Seattle.

Not expecting anyone to pick up at 4:30 in the afternoon, Marie stammered when a male voice said, "Yes."

"Ugh, I....is this officer...?"

"Drew Parish. Hello Marie." The way he said her name sent

a tingly feeling through her body. Years later she would remember that moment, and how it snagged her heart so suddenly that it caught her completely off guard. Right now, though, weary from the sleepless nights and emotional pain of watching Cynthia waste away before her eyes, she felt vulnerable as she prepared for yet another loss too painful to bear alone.

He had business in Portland and was hoping she might accept an invitation to dinner on Friday. Marie said "yes," which had surprised even her. In fact, while driving the twenty minutes it took to get home that afternoon, she tried to remember the last time she had been out with a man, but the specifics eluded her. It had been almost three years, as close as she could calculate and, up until now, it hadn't seemed like she had missed anything in life.

At her apartment, Marie immediately changed into riding clothes and rushed out the door to her car. Driving quickly but within the bounds of safety, she headed straight for Raven's Wing Horse Farm. She suddenly wanted to be with her gelding, Duke, whom she had not been able to spend much time with lately. Even if she didn't get around to actually riding today, she could take Duke out and groom him, talk to him, and ease her troubled mind of all that was rushing in on her.

CHAPTER 30

After changing three times, Marie finally put on her favorite teal-colored skirt, a loose fitting black blouse, and comfortable shoes with just enough heel to give her some height. She wore the necklace Max had given her one year for Mother's Day, a single pearl suspended from a delicate gold chain.

When Drew knocked at the door, she invited him in, fussing nervously with her purse and cell phone. His relaxed manner and flashing smile caused her even more anxiety.

"You might want to grab a sweater, it's cool out tonight," he suggested.

"Oh…" she said, turning to walk down the hall to the closet, her heels clicking on the tiled floor. When she returned, he was standing with his hands behind his back while studying the big framed group of photos hanging in the entry, pictures of Max from infancy through high school. She struggled to get into the jacket, secretly praying he wouldn't ask any questions about the photos. He turned around and helped her, an in-turned sleeve being the problem. Then he patted her on both shoulders and said, "Ready?"

She had to look away from his dark, penetrating eyes. "Mm, yea," she gulped.

In the dimly lit restaurant, Marie peered over her menu and studied Drew. His tanned face was long, the sharp cheek bones separated by a thin straight nose. His closely trimmed beard was flecked with grey hairs; the only thing about his looks that made her think he might be close to her age. He wore his hair short and slightly spiked as if he had run his fingers through it instead of a comb. Jen was right: he was a hunk of a man, except that he didn't seem to have the arrogance that often accompanied his kind of looks.

When the waiter came to take their orders, Marie said, "I'll have the same." She hadn't even read the menu. "Oh, and a glass of white Zin, please," she added. Drew ordered a beer that the waiter had recommended; it was called, 'Dog Eat Dog.' They laughed later over the bottle's label where a Chihuahua in a spiked collar, baring big white canines, stood over a cowering Pit Bull that was sweating blood.

They lingered over dinner, talking mostly about the nightmare trail ride and the up-coming trial. "That Kyle kid is doing good, you'll be glad to know. They'll likely do a plea bargain, cut him a deal in exchange for information. With Badger out of the picture, I think Kyle is relatively safe." He looked around cautiously before continuing. "That group was mostly a bunch of 'wannabe skinheads,' but they had stockpiled a virtual arsenal and a lot of drugs," he said with an undertone of disbelief.

Marie, trying to keep her emotions in check, told Drew about Cynthia's illness. He didn't just listen, he was engaged, asking pertinent questions with genuine interest and empathy. She found herself trusting him, feeling safe in his company.

"I'm going down to Salem next week, take off as much time as is necessary. I'll be there with her until..." her voice quivered, "... the end I guess."

"That's good of you. I saw a strength about you the moment we met." She looked at him, puzzled. "At your camp. That ole cowgirl might have seemed tough, but I saw fear in her," he said.

"Cyn's the strong one. You should see how she is holding her own through this. I'd be angry as hell with God if it were me," Marie said.

"The three of you have an incredible bond, don't you?"

"Yes, I suppose we do."

After a few moments of silence, as if lost in thought, Drew looked Marie in the eyes and said, "You know, I've always sort of envied women for that. I guess you have it figured out that we men are different!" He smiled, opening another door to her closed heart.

***

Most of the next morning was spent talking to Mona over the phone. Cynthia was refusing radiation and, of course, everyone had an opinion about that. The hospice nurse insisted that they all let Cyn have the freedom to make her own decisions in the closing days of her life.

"I tried to call you several times last night," Mona said. Marie didn't want to mention her date with Drew. When she didn't answer right away, Mona said, "Are you all right?"

"Yeah, I...didn't sleep well last night." She had tossed and turned like a love struck school girl, unable to get Drew out of her mind.

"I guess none of us are sleeping well these days," Mona said.

This made Marie feel like a heel. Should she be thinking about her own happiness when Cyn was facing death?

They talked about Heather and how difficult it was going to be for her. Bob was a trouper, Mona said; his only concern was making Cynthia comfortable and preparing his daughter for the impending loss of her mother. Eventually, Mona got around to saying what was really on her mind. Marie had waited patiently for her to come to that place in the conversation.

"I feel like I need to tell Cyn about what I disclosed to Heather, come clean you know? I mean, there is unfinished business between us…I think I should clear things up before it's too late." Marie made no reply. "Can you say something?" Mona asked.

"What is it you want me to say, that you were right to hold a grudge?"

"A grudge!"

"Yes, Mona. Look, no one is more opposed to abortion than I am, but you turned this into something about you, not the fetus."

Mona's voice rose in indignation, "What are you insinuating?"

"Are you sure you want to hear my opinion?"

"Of course I do," Mona insisted.

"I think you resent that Cyn has a family, a child. And she tried to cover up a terrible mistake by choosing abortion instead of life."

"That's right," Mona yelled. "It was a life, Marie."

"I agree, and what Cyn did was wrong. And she has paid for it every minute of every day since. Isn't that enough?"

Mona didn't answer right away. Marie could hear her breath catch, and sniffles through the receiver. She waited. Finally Mona's voice broke with a whining plea, "What should I do? I don't know what to do." She was crying now.

Marie drew a deep breath; her tone softened as she said, "You're doing it, Honey. You're there for her and she needs you. Let go of the rest, it doesn't matter anymore. It just doesn't."

CHAPTER 31

When they arrived at Ona Beach that first afternoon, the weather was grey and gloomy with the wind whipping at their clothes. Bob lifted Cynthia from the back seat, carried her into the beach house and settled her in an overstuffed chair, placing pillows all around her frail, thin body. Mona and Heather unpacked the car, hauling their duffle bags and groceries inside then walked down the steep steps to the low sand dunes where tall clumps of grass swayed with the gusts of wind. When Marie arrived from Portland within an hour, exhausted from the drive, she declined the invitation to join Heather and her dad for a walk down to the beach.

In spite of the wind and chill, there were numerous people combing the shore for shells and agates and half a dozen kites flying overhead. Mona went along with the two at Cynthia's insistence, giving her some private time with Marie, something she had been wanting for weeks.

This was the first time Marie remembered Cynthia ever speaking about her childhood. How she had grown up in a large family where she felt invisible: a skinny, homely girl born smack in the middle between three older brothers who resented her even having been born, and two younger twin stepsisters, that were treated special from the day they came home from the hospital. She was the designated baby sitter who seemed always in trouble with her stepfather, and told she would never amount to anything. "Girl, if you weren't so dammed ugly there might be some hope for you," he would say, humiliating her in front of her giggling siblings.

"I never felt loved," she told Marie. "Not until I met Bob." Her head turned weakly toward Marie; she wore a wry smile that was familiar to everyone who knew her.

"I kinda figured that out," Marie said. "Most really funny people are so full of shit."

"What are you saying?"

"Comedians, they're all covering up some kind of pain."

"With humor?" Cynthia asked.

"Yep. We 'comicalize.' I'm not sure if that's a word, but, it's done to distract from the ugliness around us that we have no control over."

"Oh stop! You know how I hate all that psycho-babble bullshit, Marie."

"Okay, in a nutshell…we joke to survive."

"I don't know how you deal with all those wealthy people who seem to be nothing but needy head cases. Don't you want to tell them to go get some real problems?" Cynthia said with a laugh. Marie said nothing as a silence fell between them lasting several minutes.

"I'm thinking about becoming a nun," Marie said.

"What?" Cynthia squeaked out as she broke into a coughing fit, one of the frequent symptoms of her illness. Marie grabbed the water bottle and put the straw to Cynthia's lips as she sucked weakly at the morphine-spiked liquid, the only thing that gave her limited relief from the pain that seemed to have crept into every cell of her body.

Marie looked at Cynthia's face while trying to hold her emotions in check. The cheeks were sunken, with skin sagging over bone like an old, old woman. Dark grey circles framed her eyes that amazingly still sparkled with a certain mischief.

"A nun? You don't qualify!" Cynthia said.

"Why not? I haven't been with a man in that way for several years. Did I tell you I had dinner with that helicopter hunk?"

"No!"

"Yep. And I am actually going to take him up on another such date, can you believe it?"

Cyn didn't comment and when Marie looked at her, she seemed to be in a daze. She waited in the silence until Cynthia spoke, her voice clear and devoid of humor. "I think Bob and Mona should get together when I'm gone."

"Cyn!" Marie said, stunned. "Why are you talking like…?"

"I'm dying is what's happening. It makes sense. The two have always gotten along well.

Heather needs a mom and Bob deserves a good woman. Besides, she isn't wild like me."

She smiled and winked at Marie, who felt as if something had just sucked the breath out of her. Marie strode over to the huge window overlooking the Pacific. There were big rocks along the beach to the south where waves sprayed upward a pinkish white against the horizon. The sky was a soft orange, the color of sherbet, and silhouetted against it were fishing boats slowly making their way north to the jetties where they would bring in the day's catch and begin the process all over again tomorrow.

"Who's in denial now?" Marie heard Cynthia say from her chair. It was an honest reply impossible to ignore. When she looked down, Bob was helping both Mona and Heather up the stairs that led to the beach house.

**

Dinner consisted of a tossed green salad and a delicious Chicken Alfredo sauce over fresh noodles that Marie had purchased at an Italian market in Portland. Cynthia picked at the creamy sauce with a spoon. By now she had lost her appetite completely and had to be nearly forced to drink the nutrition supplements the doctors insisted on.

Dawn, the hospice nurse, had other ideas and was all for letting a patient do whatever they wanted, even if it were refusing food or medicine. She called each night to check up on Cynthia, insisting on talking with her personally. Cynthia squealed with delight at something the nurse said and went into another coughing episode, so violent that she had to hand the phone to Bob. It was good to see the trust Cyn had in the woman: both Mona and Marie could see it was giving her a certain peace. Dawn had talked at length to Heather several times which seemed to relieve some of the earlier anxiety she had displayed toward the saddening situation.

***

The wind had died down at last; Bob lay awake next to his wife in the quiet, listening to her wheezing breath. He found himself hoping for a sunny day tomorrow so that he could take Cynthia in her wheelchair over to the bridge at Beaver Creek, where she might watch the kayakers and the abundant waterfowl. Her doctors had given her six to eight weeks to live and it was now the seventh.

Earlier that day on the beach with Mona and Heather, the loss he was facing had hit him so hard that he longed to rage like the sea, scream out into the drowning noise. And he would have if he had been alone. He even felt himself getting angry with the gulls that hopped around a dead seal with their wings out, screeching at each other and fighting over pieces of rotting flesh.

With everyone now chilled and unable to hear each other talk, he decided they should turn back toward the beach house. The cold wind stung Bob's eyes causing them to tear, but from deep down inside more came. He let them pour down his cheeks as he walked with both hands in his jacket pockets. Mona dropped back, putting her arm around Heather, as they leaned into each other for comfort.

CHAPTER 32

Drew had been calling Marie most every night since their first date and she felt herself waiting in expectation as soon as the sun went down. Tonight though, when her cell phone rang, she was reluctant to answer. She had spent most of the day washing clothes at a local laundry-mat, ridding her belongings of sand. The beach trip had been a success, a time for all of them to say goodbye to Cynthia in their own way. It seemed that something supernatural had orchestrated private moments for Cyn to spend alone with the ones closest to her.

And when they arrived home, her estranged twin sisters were waiting at the front door. Laura and Paula spent the next two days with their older sister catching up and sharing childhood memories. Cynthia's poor little body was sick but her spirit experienced a great healing. Grown women now, her sisters shed tears of regret for having let distance and differences separate them from the big sister who had taken such good care of them as children. They said their 'good bye's' when leaving, including hugs to everyone. Cynthia talked about their visit for the rest of the day, repeating funny incidents about such things as throwing the family cat from the tree house and prying bruised fingers from a mouse trap. One time, the older brothers had put dog food in Cyn's cereal and the twins cried because they thought she was dying when she fell over the toilet to puke her guts out.

On the third ring, Marie answered and was glad to hear Drew's voice. She needed to talk to someone not close to the situation with Cyn. Still, she was holding back because she really didn't know him. Sure, they were getting familiar with each other over the phone, but it was easy to speak when not making eye contact. There was something about this man that caused her to trust him more than most people she had met.

Marie had forgotten that she and Mona were supposed to be in court in less than two weeks and traveling together back to eastern Oregon for the trial. With Cynthia ill, she had lost count of the days and weeks and blanked out the trouble they had encountered with Badger. Drew informed her that the man's real name had been James Baldwin, Junior and that he was the offspring of a sixty-eight year old man, who was serving time for his involvement in a hate crime carried out by a white supremacist group out of Idaho. "I shouldn't be telling you this stuff, you've got enough to deal with right now," he said.

"No, I was face to face with that man's son. I can hear this, in fact I want to."

"All right." He cleared his throat. "Back in 1999, a couple of university students had broke down, flat tire I think. These guys stopped to help and assumed the young men were gay, beat them up, mutilated them....it was sick. The one kid died and the other one is wheelchair-bound and basically has no mind left."

Marie was silent.

"This was something you didn't need to hear …. I'm sorry," Drew said.

"I'm just tired, Drew."

"Can I help? Do you want me to drive down?"

"She has just hours left I think, not days anymore," Marie rambled.

***

The 'ting, ting, ting' of the spoon rapping against the side of the coffee mug was annoying Dawn to distraction. She reached across the table and laid her hand on Marie's wrist. Marie stared down at the deep pink nail polish and soft brown skin of the nurse's hand. Marie was afraid to look at her. Gentle finger tips lifted her chin and she found herself looking into a face of pure empathy. "Watch and listen, she's teaching you how to live."

"By dying I suppose!" Marie said, with mild sarcasm.

"YES!" she whispered. "Yes indeed child."

Suddenly Marie knew she would either cry or have to spit out what had haunted her all day. Maybe this woman could help her understand.

"Dawn, can I tell you about tapestries?"

"You mean Carol King, the singer?"

"No." Marie laughed half-heartedly. "At my mother's funeral...the priest gave an illustration about tapestries, you know the ones that hang on walls."

"Yes."

"Well, he said that this life is a tapestry, but we live on the 'back side' where all the knots that hold it together are tied ugly and look disorderly. He said we can kind of make out what the images are like: a man, a tree or a horse. But that the 'real' picture is what we will see when we get to the other side. How do you feel about that?"

"Lord, girl, that's one of the best and most comforting explanations about life this woman has ever heard! Why have you been keeping it to yourself? From now on, I'm gonna use that to help my patients. You go in there and share that with Cynthia and be holding her hand while telling it!"

And Marie did just that and she couldn't believe how well she held herself together. It seemed that Cynthia had found peace in the story of the tapestry. Marie left her sleeping with her hands folded together. Bob and Heather smiled their approval. Bob, looking haggard, didn't see Marie to the door, but Heather walked out with her. Under the porch light, Marie hugged Heather, feeling wet tears against her blouse. They all knew it was the end.

Cynthia Louise Synclair died that night while Marie was curled into a fetal position on top of her motel bed, knowing somehow that she had spent a last blessed moment with her friend. The early morning phone call was not a surprise, but the knock on her motel door ten minutes later was.

CHAPTER 33

Marie sat on the edge of the motel bed staring at the phone in her hand with a numbness laying heavily over her. Was it getting easier to have those dear to her snatched away or was she relieved that Cynthia's suffering had finally ended? It wasn't just the cancer; Cyn had been battling the guilt of her hasty abortion for a long time.

When a knock came at the door, Marie didn't get up to answer right away. Who would be looking for her at six a.m. anyway? She went to the window, pulled back the corner of the curtain, and was shocked to see Drew Parish standing there with two coffees. She slowly opened the door and unwittingly the flood gates of her emotions. Without a word, Marie turned and collapsed on the bed where she cried into a pillow for several minutes.

As he settled down next to her on the bed, she knew she needed to compose herself. When Marie opened her eyes, the white pillow case was smeared with mascara. She hadn't undressed or even washed her face the night before and realized she must look a wreck in her disheveled clothes and tear-blotched face.

"What...what are you doing here?" Marie choked out.

He tore two tissues from the box on the night stand and handed them to her. "Do you want me to leave?"

Rolling over on her side, Marie looked at him. He smiled in a teasing yet sympathetic way. A laugh escaped as she kicked at him with her bare foot. He grabbed her foot and said, "Watch it woman!" his smile belying the threat.

The revelation came as quick as the snap of a finger: that she could safely give her heart to this man; perhaps she already had without actually knowing it.

***

The community center was packed with over two hundred people in attendance for the celebration of life for Cynthia. Many of them were clients whose hair Cyn had cut, curled and colored over the years. Her twin sisters came with one of the older brothers in tow, a tall stoic man who sat alone near the door as if he might need to make a fast getaway.

An oblong table held a spray of colorful flowers around which were displayed numerous photos of Cynthia's life. There were wedding pictures of her and Bob, and later Heather as a baby, the family at Disneyland, and Christmas when Heather was growing up. And, there were the trips that the three friends had taken on horseback, caught on film. Marie couldn't imagine where they had dug it up, but a framed picture of Cynthia and Max arm-wrestling on New Year's Eve, the year before he died, stopped her heart. The memory was so clear. Max had teased Cyn, saying that she had arms like a chicken. Cynthia had looked straight at him and said, "Maxwell, I'm not sure you qualify to graduate in June if you haven't learned that chickens don't have arms, Dude!" She began flapping her arms in a silly display as Max turned red with embarrassment.

A hand touched Marie's shoulder; she turned to see Bob standing next to her. "You take that home with you," he said, looking into her moist eyes.

"Thanks Bob." He hugged her. "It was a nice service," Marie

whispered against his cheek.

"Short and sweet, just the way she wanted," he said softly.

Marie noticed that his face no longer wore the painful mask of the past few weeks while he had watched Cynthia suffer.

From across the room, she spotted Heather who had been glued to Mona the entire day. Marie then found Drew and watched as he assisted an elderly lady get seated then help with her plate of food. The two were laughing as he hung her cane on the back of the chair. Not only is he handsome, she thought, but also a good man. At the beach house when Marie had told Cynthia that she had gone on a date with the 'helicopter' guy, Cyn had made the comment that he was 'yummy.'

Marie burst out laughing, "Yummy?"

"Yep, yummy!" Cyn said, winking weakly at Marie.

She would miss her quirky little friend, who had insisted that risking a broken heart was nothing compared to the death sentence she had been given.

Oh, how fragile life is, fragile and uncertain.

CHAPTER 34

"Thank God!" Marie said out loud, as she pressed the 'end' button on her cell phone. She supposed Mona would receive the same phone call informing her that she would also not be required to testify at the trial after all. Later that day when she spoke with Drew Parish, he informed her that the case had been moved to Pendleton. The deposition Mona and Marie had given had apparently been enough.

"I've been in contact with Della Frost throughout this whole ordeal," he said. "By the way, she has retrieved all the belongings that were left up at camp when you had to hightail it out of there."

"Wow," Marie said quietly. "I had forgotten all about that stuff."

"I have a proposal for you, Marie. How about taking a little road trip?"

"Huh?" she said, having taken her own mental trip back to that last ride with Cyn and Mona and the trail guide from Hell.

"Well," he continued. "I have to…you see it's that the investigation has wound down and these guys think they need to drill me on some details before I go up against the defense. It's complicated, Marie." She sensed the frustration in his tone. "I would enjoy your company if you would like to ride over with me." He cringed inwardly knowing she would likely decline. Her silence seemed to carry its own answer. "I'm making you uncomfortable, aren't I?" he asked.

"No, no! It's just that...I was thinking about all that unfolded that week of the ride. Seems rather surreal, as if it never really happened."

"Della would like to see you; she's offered to let us stay there. Separate rooms, of course," he quickly added.

"You two buddies now?" Marie asked playfully. When Drew laughed into her ear it sounded like music to her battered soul. Holy Jesus, she thought, what is this man doing to me?

***

The quiet in the truck cab felt natural to Marie as she glanced over at Drew's hands on the steering wheel, tanned and beautiful in a masculine sort of way. She had agreed to accompany him to eastern Oregon under the condition that she would not have to go to Pendleton with him. She would stay at the ranch and visit with Della while catching up on some of the work she had neglected too long. The required paper work and the responsibilities connected to dispensing medications were the worst burdens of her profession, and had little to do with her being a therapist.

As the sun warmed the interior of Drew's truck, Marie was enveloped in a peace she couldn't remember feeling for a very long time. The subtle scent of cologne made her feel heady and, when she looked over at his hands again, she wondered what it would be like to feel them touch her for more than those swift moments when he had helped with her jacket or guided her through a restaurant door. Unconsciously she sighed aloud.

Drew looked over at her. "Need a coffee?" he asked.

"Sure. That sounds good actually." She smiled at him, and then, unable to bear his penetrating eyes, she bent down to retrieve her large purse and pulled out a bag of gourmet jelly beans just as he was pulling into a roadside mini mart. When he returned with the coffees and a couple of water bottles, he found Marie picking through the jelly beans. She looked much too serious.

"Find a bug in there or something?" he asked.

When she looked up, his head was tilted with curiosity. "No, I was looking for the popcorn flavored ones, here," she said, offering him the bag of candy.

"Nooo thank you, I mean, all the different flavors. Those things are an assault on the taste buds in my opinion."

"And you, Mister Parish, are an assault on the senses," Marie said, suddenly shocked at her own boldness.

Her abruptness must have set him back as well, because he didn't seem to know what to say or where to put the items in his hands. Marie reached over for the drinks and set them in the console while avoiding eye contact. Then, Drew Parish closed the driver side door, walked around to her door and opened it. He cleared his throat, licked his lips and took Marie's face in his hands. He looked straight into her eyes and said, "I'm in love with you, Marie." Then he kissed her, deeply. Nothing like the small pecks on the cheek she had become accustomed to from him. Two teenage girls giggled from the sidewalk as they walked huddled together glancing back toward the truck. Marie stuck her tongue out at them.

This guy is serious, she thought. He'd started talking about his past life as soon as they got back on the road; and by the time Marie saw the sign for the town of Willow Forks she felt like she had taken a crash course in 'Drew Parish 101.' She didn't mind, he had obviously never told his whole story to anyone and he wasn't looking for any sympathy. At one point she went into therapist mode and said, "Are you unloading on me because you know I'm a doctor?"

"Hell no, Marie, I want you to know who I am. I want to make you a part of my life if you'll let me."

CHAPTER 35

Della Frost greeted Marie warmly and hugged Drew like a long lost friend. Then turning to Marie, her look grew sympathetic as she said, "I'm truly sorry about your little blond friend."

"Thank you," Marie said, averting her eyes when she felt her emotions rise up. Was it this place, the last memories made here with Cyn, or was it the huge load of information Marie had just been given by Drew that made her want to cry?

Drew stepped in front of them to open the door to the ranch house, and once again they were treated to the tantalizing smells of home cooking. Within fifteen minutes they were seated at the kitchen table with baked chicken, mashed potatoes and several home-canned vegetables steaming in front of them. While Marie ate as if it were her only meal in days, Drew and Della caught up on all the details of the investigation and the trial that would start in just two days. When Kyle's name came up, Marie was all ears and Drew, looking over at her knowingly, told her what he knew she would feel relieved about. Kyle's attorney would plea bargain in order for him to receive a lighter sentence, and he would likely do a lot of community service instead of jail time. "The kid is guilty mainly by association and was ignorant of most of what Badger was involved with. They found only small traces of marijuana in his system when he was tested at the hospital and, for all it's worth because it can't be used in court, he did pass the lie detector tests."

The back door opened just as Marie got up to excuse herself and Sully came sauntering in, looking tired but smiling as he eyed the food on the table. He hung his dirty hat on a hook and started to sit down.

"Get over to the sink and wash those hands mister!" Della said.

"But I had gloves on miss…"

"Never mind that, wash up you old buzzard or you'll not be sittin' at this table tonight," she warned, grinning playfully at her guests.

"I'd better say goodnight," Marie said, adding that she was tired.

Drew scooted his chair back. "Then, I'd better get your bags."

She didn't realize how exhausted she was until she began to climb the steep old stairwell.

"Goodnight Marie," Della's voice came from the kitchen.

"Thanks Della, for everything." And that was about all Marie remembered until she awoke in the middle of the night unable to go back to sleep.

CHAPTER 36

The safety light from the barn washed over the room in a yellow haze as Marie's mind picked through the details from that day when Drew had shared his life with her. He had grown up near Yuma, Arizona, where his father had been a border patrol agent and where his mother still lived on the family ranch. She was a tall, Spanish beauty whose passion for horses was rivaled only by the fierce love she held for her husband and sons. On the day agents came to tell her of her husband's death, Drew was helping his mother saddle a young horse in the round pen. When they suggested that the 'boy' be sent to the house, Drew's mother said, "My son is a man, we hide nothing from him." Drew was sixteen and, although his father had talked at length with the family about the dangers associated with his job, nothing could have prepared them for such a tragedy. Drug traffickers had gunned down Drew's father and two fellow officers. They were arrested three days later at a cock fight by under cover officers after bragging about the 'pinche puercos' they had left to rot in the desert.

Soon after turning eighteen, Drew Parish entered the Marine Corps where he quickly gained the respect of his comrades and superiors alike. His military life was cut short though when he returned from the Middle East a decorated, severely wounded soldier. A comminuted fracture to the femur requiring three surgeries took nearly three years to heal and left him wondering what he would do with the rest of his life.

During Drew's long recovery, he met and married his dentist's assistant. One year later, she gave birth to the daughter of his dreams and then promptly left him for another man. To combat his feelings of inadequacy, Drew entered a phase that could only be seen by Marie as over-achievement to compensate for his assumed failures. His new career as a S.W.A.T. team member had taken him all over the country, leaving little time to connect with his daughter. He regretted that chapter of his life and assured Marie that he was very close to Misty, who was now a twenty-two-year-old woman.

Crawling back into bed, Marie snuggled down against the soft mattress, so used to curling into a ball of comfort intended to make her feel whole. She reached out and laid her palm down on the cool sheet, the empty spot next to her that could be filled if she would only open her heart, extend herself, and trust Drew Parish.

Wind rattled the old window as if to shake Marie from her musings. She got up from the bed and sat in the wing back chair; outside an owl was perched on a tree branch just an arm's length away. His head turned slowly to reveal a pair of penetrating yellow eyes circled in black. Somewhere in the distance a horse whinnied. The owl dropped, with wings spread as he floated out over the barn and into the darkness.

Leaning back with her eyes closed, Marie thought about her resolve to remain single and how quickly it was fading. Drew had been married and now had a daughter living in Tucson. Marie had lost a son. Knowing she had put Max first in her life, to the extent that there seemed to be no room for a soul mate, regret tugged at her heart. Therapists had their own demons to expel, this she knew all too well.

CHAPTER 37

The woodpecker was pecking louder and louder; through the mist Marie could make out its red head. She was dreaming, and when she opened her eyes she realized the knocking was at her door. Coming fully awake, Marie sat up in bed and said, "Come in."

The door opened slowly as Drew poked his head in, "Did I wake you?" He entered the room with a steaming cup of coffee before she could answer.

"You are always bringing me coffee, Mr. Parish."

He smiled and said, "I wouldn't mind being the one to bring you coffee every morning for the rest of your life."

Marie avoided his eyes as he handed her the mug; she knew her face must be scarlet, not to mention bare of make-up. She self-consciously ran her hand through her muddled hair and cleared her throat as he sat in the chair nearby. In contrast, he was showered, smelling of whatever intoxicating cologne he always wore and dressed in a shimmering grey suit with a maroon tie hanging loosely around his neck. She wondered if he had any idea just how good looking he was at that moment.

"I've got to get on the road," he said, glancing at his watch.

"I'll be gone two nights but back in time for the branding."

They were both looking forward to it, knowing dozens of local ranchers showed up to help at these events, where the beer flowed in buckets after all the hard work was done, and the smell of sweating horses and burned hide was usually replaced by a tri-tip barbeque, as everyone enjoyed the satisfaction of hard work and shared camaraderie.

"I hope you get some time to unwind here, but I'll miss you," Drew said. He came over to the bed, touched Marie's face with the back of his hand then bent and kissed the top of her head. Then he headed for the door, calling back to her, "See you in a couple of days."

When Marie heard his diesel truck start up, she whispered, "Traveling mercies Mr. Parish."

***

It was a beautiful October morning as the sun filled the front porch where Marie sat with her warmed up plate of scrambled eggs and toast. Della was off somewhere on the ranch, leaving her alone at the house. The peace and tranquility of the moment engulfed Marie as her thoughts turned to the future. She knew that city life had never appealed to her, but her pride had kept her from admitting that she was tired of the career she had so doggedly chased after for years. Where had it gotten her? Yes, she enjoyed the people she worked with, yet knew none of them well enough to call a true friend. They had kids or spouses, busy lives filled with other people that they loved. She thought, too, of the many affluent patients she had treated, who seemed as addicted to therapy as they were to the possessions and prescription drugs that could never fulfill them. There were those individuals who seemed resilient and didn't stay in therapy long. They were the few who she supposed had kept her hopeful, until lately.

Her thoughts were interrupted by voices as a man and woman came around the corner of the house with Rolex following at their heels. She hadn't seen the dog since arriving and was happy when he came bounding toward her in apparent recognition. "Rolex, you old scoundrel. How ya been?" She hugged him as he laid his head in her lap licking at her hands. When Marie looked up, she was surprised to see Bev standing there with a rugged looking cowboy whose bottom lip protruded from a mass of chewing tobacco tucked in tight. Bev shifted her weight from one side to the other and looked as if she had something she wanted to say.

"I'll just leave you two alone, got some chores to attend to anyways," the man said in a deep voice. He patted Bev on the shoulder. She looked at him pleadingly and reached up to touch his hand. He stomped down the steps, adjusted his worn Stetson and began whistling what Marie thought was the tune to 'You are my Sunshine…' Rolex trotted along beside him.

"Sit down Bev," Marie said, pointing to a nearby wicker chair. She noticed how much better Bev looked since the last time she had seen her, when they had left her drunk and passed out by the side of the trail. Her hair was layered in a feminine cut and she wore an attractive, silky bandana around her neck, above a western shirt with a rose pattern and pearl snaps up the front.

"I ain't lookin' fer no therapy…" Bev said matter-of-factly as she sat on the edge of the chair.

"And I ain't offering none," Marie said, smiling at the woman. Bev seemed to relax at Marie's humor and sincerity.

"I got all yer stuff boxed up that was left up there…at camp. Sorry 'bout yer friend too…I mean it."

"Of course you do Bev, look we…"

"No. I got somethin' to say and I best do it now 'cause I might chicken out, so listen up, okay?"

"Sure Bev."

"I screwed up, up there and I'm sayin' sorry for it. I been learnin' in A.A. and I hope you'll figure a way to forgive me… someday."

They fell into an awkward silence, until Marie noticed Bev

squirming uncomfortably and said, "How about today, sound good to you?" She got up and put out her hand. Bev stared for a few seconds before reaching out to take her offer. She smiled at Marie and blinked several times, tears welling up in her eyes.

As she lifted Bev's hand, Marie saw a small gold band with three tiny diamonds, "What's this—a ring?" she asked. She also took note that Bev's nails, although short, were clean and polished a soft pink.

"Kinda old to be gettin' a 'promise' ring I reckon," Bev said, with a mix of pride and embarrassment.

"Nonsense!" Marie hugged her ever-so-slightly around the shoulders. "Congratulations cowgirl."

"Ha!"

To Marie, that sounded like happiness.

CHAPTER 38

Forcing herself to go back indoors, Marie left the comfort of the sunny porch to tidy up the kitchen for Della. Then she reluctantly made her way up to the room and her lap-top. As much as she would have liked to, she could not put off the work-related responsibilities that awaited attention. Two and a half hours later, with an aching neck and fuzzy brain from too much concentration, Marie decided she needed a break. Aside from that, she could hear activity going on down below, voices and laughter that made her feel like she was missing out on something.

There was a sudden 'clump, clump' outside her door and then a sniffing noise. When Marie opened the door, Rolex had his nose stuffed in the corner. He looked up at her sheepishly then squeezed through the door and began inspecting all of Marie's belongings. His stub of a tail waggled back and forth as he smelled her pillow, bags and then drooled all over the case of her lap-top.

"Everything meet your approval, sir?" she said to the dog. He walked to the door and stood waiting for her. "I'm coming! Mind if I get my hat first?" She patted Rolex on his silky head. "You came up here to get me, didn't you boy?"

Della bustled about the kitchen making sandwiches while Sully, Bev, and the man who had been with her that morning sat at the table talking.

"Number thirty three is missing, the one with a bad hip," Bev was saying.

"Likely got killed by a cougar," Sully said. He leaned back in his chair, arms folded over his chest.

"Could be, could be," Della said. She turned around and pointed the mayonnaise-covered knife in Sully's direction. "But, if you recall, that heifer is always one of the last to come down."

"True enough, ma'am."

Della spotted Marie in the doorway and smiled. "C'mon in, we're fixin' to have us some lunch."

Marie offered to help.

"Sure. Put these sandwiches on the table and I'll get the rest of the trappings."

She gave Marie a motherly pat on the shoulder. It was so seldom anyone touched her and Marie, knowing the importance of the human touch, felt an instant longing for that missing ingredient in her life.

Besides sandwiches, there were bags of chips, canned pears, pickles, and a plate of sliced cheeses added to the table. A big pot of homemade chicken soup was steaming in the center as Della dipped the ladle, filling the bowls generously. Rolex stared at them pleadingly from his spot on a rug, knowing better than to beg.

"Have you met Will?" Della asked, as she gestured toward the man Marie had seen with Bev that morning.

"We've not been formally introduced." She extended her hand. "Hello Will, I'm Marie Geracie, nice to meet you."

"Ma'am," he said with a nod of his head as he grasped her hand tightly.

Della never sat down, leaning instead against the sink where she took bites of her sandwich while going over details and assigning tasks for the day's activities. "We're headed up to the holding pens to set up for the branding. You're welcome to tag along if you'd like," she told Marie.

"Sounds good to me, but please give me something physical to do. All I've done is exercise my brain this morning."

***

It was a beautiful drive along the rough, dusty road. Cottonwoods were beginning to turn yellow with the chill of autumn nights. Surprised by a herd of thirteen Big Horn sheep, Della stopped for Marie to get a couple of close photos before they scrambled up a rocky ravine and disappeared from sight. Behind them, Bev and Will sat close, kissing in the cab of the truck, missing the sheep altogether.

"Jis' look at them two," Sully said. "Couldn't put a knife between 'em, even if it were greased with butter!"

"Well now Sullivan McBain, am I sensing a tad bit of jealousy on your part?" Della teased. "Ya know, if you weren't so hell bent on staying a bachelor, you might just find you a nice gal to saddle up with."

Sully huffed, mumbled something under his breath and stared out the windshield at the road in front of them.

"This here is Echo Springs," Della said as she pulled the big truck up next to a loading chute. There were cattle in the pens mulling around, licking at the molasses supplement tubs used to lure them into the enclosure.

Marie took in the incredible surroundings, feeling as if she had been dropped off into a small paradise. A doe with two half grown fawns grazed along the edges of a crystal clear pool of water that was fed by a waterfall that tumbled down over a natural rock wall about fifty feet above. Nearby, a stone fireplace, its chimney still intact, stood as a lone sentinel where, Marie was told, homesteaders had been burned out during the Indian wars before the turn of the century. A small rose bush held several red roses as it clung to the corner stone of what had once been a home.

Bev and Will parked their trailer and unloaded the two

horses they would be using to try and find the stray cattle left in the hills. They were camping there for the night while Della, Sully and Marie would return to the ranch. Everyone worked hard together unloading hay bales, sleeping gear, picnic tables, firewood, and the many supplies that would be needed for a day of branding.

Feeling pleasantly exhausted, Marie climbed into the pick-up for the long drive back to the ranch, her thoughts on Drew and how much she found herself missing him.

CHAPTER 39

Marie declined when offered dinner that evening, saying she was too tired to eat and needed a hot shower more than food. The conversation on the way back down from Echo Springs was still fresh in her mind and had been a bit unsettling. Why it mattered now she didn't know. Sully had told Marie that the best way to "Git a bullet straight to a horse's brain is to shoot them in the eye or the ear." He said Cynthia was lucky it hadn't bounced right off Smokey's frontal plate and possibly injured or even killed her. Della's silence seemed to confirm what he'd said.

The next morning, Marie was awakened by a light tapping on the bedroom door. Della opened the door ajar and said, "Mornin' gal, you have a phone call." Marie knew it was Drew by the twinkle in the woman's eyes. Trying not to seem too anxious, Marie pulled a sweatshirt on over her head and headed slowly downstairs where Della was chatting away until she saw Marie. "Well, you tell Kyle he's got himself a job here when the dust settles on this rodeo. Here's yer gal."

As she took the phone in her hands, Marie felt her palms getting clammy. "Hello Marie darling, I trust you slept well last night," he said cheerfully.

Marie laughed. "Is this Prince Drew perchance?"

"'Tis I!"

"Cut it out Shakespeare." She heard him take a deep breath.

"I miss you, Marie."

'Trust him,' she was telling herself when Della appeared with a cup of coffee and placed it on a coaster. Marie mouthed 'Thank you.'

Drew asked, "Are you there?"

"Yes, I'm here...and...I miss you Drew. How's the trial going?"

"We're pretty pleased, better than we expected." He told her he wouldn't be able to make it back to the ranch until early the next morning because he had some shopping to do in Pendleton. To hide her disappointment, Marie said she had some more work-related duties to take care of anyway.

It turned out she didn't accomplish much as the day progressed, so she gave up and closed her laptop in frustration. After finding the big house empty of bodies, Marie walked down to the barnyard, where there was quite a commotion going on inside one of the corrals. Four spindly little legs with hooves the size of a silver dollar, were sticking straight up out of a feeding trough. Everyone was shouting orders as Bev and Will tried to pull the foal out, but every time they touched the animal's legs, its flailing hooves proved impossible to hold onto.

When Sully looked up at Marie, sweat pouring down his face, she said, "Could we all get on one side and maybe tip the trough over?"

Everyone looked at her. They were out of breath and near panic. "That's the best darned idea yet," Sully said. Mud was caked around the bottom and Will had to chop at it with a shovel to break it loose. The mare stood in a corner of the corral, nickering nervously as she watched them with wild eyes. "On a count of three," Della ordered. "One, two, three!"

Shouts rose up as the trough rolled over and the foal

immediately scrambled out, rushing to its mothers side, where it pushed beneath her flank and began to nurse.

***

Marie had overslept and was about to head down to the kitchen when Drew surprised her at the top of the stairs. Taking her into his arms, he held her for a long moment before releasing his hold. Their eyes met briefly before he kissed her softly on the lips and then whispered against her cheek, "It's so good to see you."

Marie felt a lump in her throat; she wanted to cry but, not knowing why, she wondered if she felt undeserving of this man's love or afraid of it. Della broke the spell by shouting up to them that they would be pulling out in fifteen minutes. "You two 'love birds' better get down here and pull yer weight or I'll put ya to work mendin' fences."

The ranch yard was full of pick-ups, the beds piled high with ice chests, saddles, kids, and cow dogs that never seemed to stop barking. From trailers behind them, horses whinnied back and forth and stomped impatiently. As the caravan began to pull out, Drew and Marie waited in his truck until the last rig left. They followed far behind to avoid the dust and to savor the privacy and company. Several times, Drew reached over to squeeze Marie's hand and was rewarded by an approving smile.

"I can't believe I'm here with you. I feel so...content." He didn't know he had stolen the words Marie wished she could say herself. She knew in her heart that his warmth would eventually open her up like a stubborn bud needing to flower.

***

At the branding site, they were caught up in the organized chaos and saw very little of one another for most of the day. Drew plunged right in, offering his help and taking in stride the relentless jibes from well-meaning cowboys. Della let everyone know that, although Drew Parish hadn't been around cattle ranching much, he and his mother had raised and trained some of the finest Spanish horses this side of Mexico.

All morning Marie watched as little boys in boots and over-sized cowboy hats climbed in and out of truck beds and over fences, hiding from the girls whose ponytails they had yanked on or necks they had thrown a lasso around. She helped to settle a near fist fight between two ten- year olds and rocked more than one baby to sleep. By the middle of the day, with calves bawling, choking dust, and the stench of burned hide hanging in the air, the sudden threat of rain was a welcome sight.

An elderly man who had attached himself to Marie held a tarp over them as a soft rain fell for the next five minutes. "Stick around for a minute and the weather is likely to change," he said with a chuckle. Marie soon knew all about 'Pete,' his time in Korea, the grandson that had died in Afghanistan and whose ashes were scattered in Wild Horse Meadows, and how he was afraid that ranching was soon going to be a thing of the past.

Late in the afternoon with the branding completed, it became 'adult' time as coolers were opened up and beers passed around. The laughter grew louder as a group of men stood arguing around the flaming barbeque pit.

"Ah to hell with that 'mon tree all' crap, where's 'mon tree all' anyways? It ain't in 'merica by God!"

"Montreal. It's in Canada, you idiot," a woman shouted. She stood with her arms folded, watching with obvious irritation as the man twirled a steak around on the end of a long fork and then dropped it in the dirt; that caused a hearty round of rib jabbing and laughter among the onlookers.

"Shit Arn, look what ya did," another bystander said, as he reached down and picked it up. He took off his bandana and wiped the steak off then handed it to a boy standing nearby. "Go wash this off in the spring, kid."

"All's we need is some wes...westersheer sauce, nothin' more," he started in again.

The woman, who had apparently had enough, pushed through the crowd and confronted him. "I'll tell you someone who don't need nothin' more to drink." She pulled a set of keys out of her pocket and dangled them in front of him. "I'm leavin' Arnie, and you can find yer own damned ride home."

As she turned on her heels and strode away, she added, "Next week would be too soon for me! Get yer ass in the truck, Junior!" she said to one of the boys who Marie had earlier stopped from fighting. No wonder the kid had some pent up anger, she thought.

Next to her, Bev sipped on a lemon lime soda. "Makes ya wonder where that's gonna end up," Bev said under her breath.

CHAPTER 40

Drew was acting rather curious. Marie had seen him and Della whispering to each other as the crew gathered into their perspective groups to eat at the long line of picnic tables. When she passed a bowl of potato salad to him, he was exchanging a glance with Bev who looked like the cat that had swallowed the canary. Something was up, and Marie sensed that it had to do with her.

Bracing herself for a practical joke, she was about to question Drew, when he suddenly asked, "Marie, would you mind getting my coat for me? It's on the hood of my truck."

Dumbstruck, Marie just stared at him. "Your coat?" she said. "You want me to get your coat?"

"Yes. It's rather chilly out, don't you think?"

"No, it's not ch—" she started.

"Oh sure it is!" Della said from across the table as several people chimed in with, "Ugh huh," and "Yes," and "It's chilly alright."

Marie got up and walked toward the truck. What else could she do when he had put her on the spot? People stood up and were whispering amongst each other and then they began to follow her. As she approached the truck, she could see there was no coat but she did spot a small black, velvet box. And scrawled into the thick dust on the hood were the words, "Will you marry me?"

Paralyzed for what seemed like eternity, Marie waited and then she felt Drew's arms around her. Tears streamed down her cheeks and an overwhelming sensation came over her, so powerful that she thought it might cause her heart to explode.

"Well?" He was looking into her eyes and all she could think was, 'Say it, say it!' The soft roll of thunder in the distance broke through her thoughts as if granting permission.

"Yes," she said quietly.

"What did she say?" the crowd called out.

"Yes!" she said again, louder.

Suddenly the two were surrounded by people hugging Marie, shaking Drew's hand, and patting him on the back while making off-color jokes about sex.

"Hey now, knock it off! This here's a lady and ya better watch yer mouths!" Bev hollered. She turned to Marie, "I'm real happy for ya, Miss Marie." She nodded toward Drew, "You and him."

***

That school girl, butterflies-in-her-stomach feeling had stayed with Marie all the way home from Willow Forks and she couldn't stop staring down at the diamond ring encircled by more tiny diamonds and four small emeralds. Everyone at the branding had oohed and ahhed over it when Drew had proudly slipped it on her finger. She wanted so badly to call Mona and share the news but something held her back. She had not talked to Mona for weeks and had given up trying to contact her at home. Since Cyn's death, their friendship seemed to have been put on hold and Marie wondered if it would ever return to normal. The element of humor that had been a buffer between the three strong-willed women was now missing, along with Cyn.

Thinking maybe she should call Bob to see if he might know why Mona had been so hard to track down, Marie picked up the phone then immediately decided against it. Instead, she poured herself a glass of Merlot, grabbed the thick stack of mail from the kitchen counter and headed for her bedroom. With a half dozen pillows propped around her on the bed, she began sorting the mail like a deck of cards into separate piles. There was a mountain of junk mail, magazines, a letter from Aunt Rhoda who wrote faithfully every month with all the gossip from the nursing home; a free sample of laundry soap and another personal letter in the old-fashioned, standard-sized envelope from Mona Sinclair....Sinclair.

"Sinclair!" Marie said out loud.

Staring across the room at the black television screen, Marie sat frozen in place, her stomach knotted as tears of shock and anger dripped onto the letter. Wiping them with the back of her shaking hand, she grabbed the wine glass and gulped down the entire contents then got up and paced the room, avoiding the letter that lay on the night stand. The room was beginning to darken as the sun set outside; reaching for the empty glass and letter, Marie walked down the dim hallway to the kitchen, where she flipped on the switch for the chandelier over the dining room table. As she poured another glass of wine and sat down, she had a vision of Cynthia that caused goose bumps to form on her arms. "Cowboy up," she could hear her friend saying as she winked, the little laugh lines appearing across her face.

A photo fell from the open letter, landing face up on the table. Bob was in the middle with Mona on one side and Heather on the other; there were palm trees in the background.

Dear Marie,

I know you will be angry and hurt by this letter, for which I am truly sorry. We realize that you may feel that it is too soon after the loss of Cyn for Bob and me to marry. We went to Las Vegas for a private ceremony with only Heather accompanying us. Heather is happy that we have become a family, which is what matters most I'm sure you will agree. It is my hope that you will come to understand and be happy for me, for us, too.

Always, Mona

CHAPTER 41

Marie thought that calling Drew to complain about Mona's hasty marriage would gain her some sympathy, but she was wrong. He told her that she should be happy for her friend; yes, it may be untimely by Marie's calendar, but Cynthia herself had wished for this very thing and had not attached a particular date as to when it would be appropriate.

Still sobbing into her pillow three hours after hanging up on Drew, Marie heard the door bell ring. She could see him through the peep hole and reluctantly opened the door. It only took looking into his eyes to soften her.

That night, Marie cried a river of tears as Drew held her close, while all the pain that had been damned up inside finally broke loose. Her lonely childhood, Max's father leaving her, losing Max and then Cyn, and how she knew she had become a therapist because she thought she could somehow 'fix' the world that was so very broken.

As they lay together on top of the bed still fully clothed, with the sun beginning to light the room, Marie said, "Guess we had our first quarrel, huh?"

"Yes, and there will be more I'm sure."

Marie sighed. "I hate to be so humble. It's not in my nature ya know? But, you were right Drew."

"I haven't told you anything you didn't already know."

"I'm sorry," she said.

"I know." He had figured out months ago that Marie was the kind of woman to be handled like a spirited horse, firm, but gentle enough not to break her will. That spirit was the part of her he loved most.

EPILOGUE

Marie, Mona and Heather huddled together on a crisp autumn morning in northeastern Washington State, as they watched the sign go up for the 'Copper Creek Boys Ranch.' From tall ladders Bob and Drew secured the engraved board to the Tamarack entry, while Kyle lowered the tractor's bucket and gave them all a 'thumbs up' before heading for the barn. He was anxious to shower and be on his way to the airport in Spokane where Drew's daughter, Misty, was flying in from Phoenix. The two of them had hit it off immediately the previous Christmas, when Drew and Marie were married in a simple ceremony, next to the big stone fireplace at the Frost Ranch.

Had it been almost a year? Marie couldn't believe it. So much had changed, and now she found herself embarking on a whole new life so different from anything she had ever imagined. Marie had given up her practice with no regrets and gifted her beloved 'Duke' to Mona who, in turn, handed Lark over to Heather as her own personal mount. Drew and Marie decided to keep Marie's condo for a winter place, when the boys' ranch would be buried in snow and closed for the season.

Kyle would return in the spring to work assisting the Activities Director and help Marie with the horse program as part of his probation. It had taken some effort on Drew's part to convince the authorities, and now he and Marie were determined that Kyle would be one of the success stories. Marie had also hired Cora, now a trusted friend, who was a nutritionist and would be the main cook for the nine teenage boys arriving in the spring.

Drew, on the other hand, seemed to be a mystery to everyone. He was still a Swat Team member but had recently started working with the Canadian border patrol—his assignment top secret. He had gone to great lengths to make Marie's dream of the boys' ranch a reality. His devotion and hard work made her love him even more. And although she would always worry about his safety, she knew he was a soldier first, and that his need to serve others had won not only her heart, but her respect and admiration.

Acknowledgments

Many thanks to my editor Sandy Raschke for her patience and promptings as well as praise and for all she has taught me throughout this process.

Thank you members of the River Valley Writers Group, Eloise Boren at E.R. Printing and Graphics, and the many friends, teachers and acquaintances who, over the years, have encouraged me in ways they may not have been aware of.

Without the support of my children, Sarah, Rachael, Nathan and Keegan, my husband Todd, and extended family, this dream would never have become a reality. Thanks for believing in me.

Last, I thank my 'sister' friends; we might not come from the same family, but are related through our shared memories and experiences, be they painful or pleasurable.